The Amir

The Tora Bora Vendetta

Dean Davidson

Table of Contents

Copyright	1
Preface	2
Acknowledgements	6
Dedications	7
Chapter 1	8
Chapter 2	16
Chapter 3	27
Chapter 4	37
Chapter 5	45
Chapter 6	52
Chapter 7	60
Chapter 8	68
Chapter 9	77
Chapter 10	84
Chapter 11	91
Chapter 12	100
Chapter 13	107
Chapter 14	116
Chapter 15	122
Chapter 16	128
Chapter 17	133
Chapter 18	137
Chapter 19	141
Chapter 20	145
Chapter 21	149
Chapter 22	154
Chapter 23	159
Chapter 24	166
Epilogue	168

Copyright

Published by Defiance Press & Publishing, LLC

Bulk orders of this book may be obtained by contacting Defiance Press & Publishing, LLC. www.defiancepress.com.

Defiance Press & Publishing, LLC
281-581-9300
info@defiancepress.com

Preface

I served during the Cold War era and was never deployed to a combat area of operation.

During my second year stationed in Germany in the 1980s, my commander called me into his office and told me to go to the Kaserne theater early the following morning.

This was common at the time for random drug screens.

The following morning, my buddy and I were both seated in the theater along with two soldiers from each of the four companies on our Kaserne.

What we all assumed was a random drug test turned out to be something the Army called “inter-theater recruiting” for the Special Forces.

The program was specific to the Green Berets and focused on qualified soldiers volunteering for Special Forces selection training, or what was called Special Forces Assessment and Selection (SFAS).

I was an E-4 with a 76Y MOS, Unit Supply Specialist.

Earlier that year, I had been selected to attend the SaM-31 Advanced Small Arms Training school in Vilksek, Germany. I was an E-3 (Private First Class) at the time. The rest of the class consisted of E-7s, a lieutenant, warrant officers, and one E-5.

It was a two-week course, and my First Sergeant told me before I left that if I didn’t pass, not to bother coming back to the unit.

The E-5 and I were the only two to graduate from the course on the first attempt. The rest of the class had to stay an extra couple of days for a refresher and retake the test.

I was not an exceptional soldier. I didn't max out my P.T. scores. I maxed out push-ups and sit-ups, but I was a terrible runner; I always have been. But I had grit and determination. I didn't back down from a fight, and I worked hard to prove others wrong while also doing what I could to help my team. Maybe that's why I was selected to attend the recruitment meeting.

Joining Special Forces had always been my dream as a kid. Pretending to be Zorro or James Bond, taking down the bad guys to help save others. All I needed to do was attend the PLDC (Primary Leadership Development Course) and wait for the next open selection training date.

Sadly, for me, that opportunity would never materialize.

I had a Top-Secret NATO clearance at the time I learned my stepfather was under investigation by the FBI, which could potentially interfere with my clearance. My stepfather was a bit of a hippie liberal. He had followed the Grateful Dead during college and written articles for Rolling Stone Magazine.

He was an idealist, always against "the man." He and our pastor made trips down to El Salvador to help those trying to flee to safety cross the border into Mexico and later into the United States. I don't know all the details, but I assume they were helping them cross into the U.S. illegally.

Due to his activities and the FBI investigation, I declined the opportunity to attend SFAS.

I convinced myself that it would be a blight on my record and would keep me from selection, even if I had completed the course.

Many years later, I found myself working for and running day-to-day operations for a small international security firm.

I had grown the security services side of the business to include security personnel and drivers for celebrities and high-value personnel around the world.

One of the corporations I was trying to bring on board as a client was an international shipping company that wanted to re-evaluate their onboard security policies. They were currently using Gurkhas, the

Nepalese soldiers, on their ships in specific locations around the world. They felt it was overkill and wanted someone to conduct a quiet assessment without the crew being made aware.

I was aware of Commander Marcinko's reputation and his creation of what was called Red Cell. I immediately felt that was the approach this client needed to accomplish their required assessment.

Through some of my other business efforts, I had been fortunate enough to be introduced to one of the original Team Six members, Chris Caracci. He turned out to be one of the nicest people I had ever met.

Chris helped me reach out to Dick and coordinated with another former Team Six member, Dan Capel, to work out a plan for a meeting with the client at their offices in Norfolk, VA.

Dick invited me to stay at his home before the meeting.

I was a little gobsmacked, to be honest. I was a nobody. No combat experience. I hadn't gone through selection; I was just an average guy with enough courage to have called on the founder of Seal Team Six to join me in a sales meeting. And here I was, breaking bread with the man in his home.

That deal didn't pan out, but I did end up working with Dan to help conduct the first private security detail in Lagos, Nigeria, for Continental Airlines when they were putting together non-stop services from Houston to Lagos.

Later that year, I also met another former UDT and SEAL Team member, whom I am grateful to consider a friend: Ron Relf. Ron has a storied career in the teams, as well as the CIA and as a former SWAT member of a western police department.

The inspiration for the main character of this book, John Spencer, is loosely based on Ron's career. Ron is a man of honor, and I consider myself better for knowing him.

Another person I consider a friend and the inspiration for the supporting character of this book, Benham Abbasi, is a man known to some as the Chinese-Mexican: Changiz Lahidji.

Changiz served in the U.S. Army ODA for more than twenty years and is considered the longest-serving member of the U.S. Special Forces A-teams in history.

I met Changiz in Kabul, Afghanistan, while working on a Special Forces contract: the training and mentoring program for the Afghan Commando Kandaks.

In my opinion, I don't deserve to even know these men, let alone be blessed enough to consider some of them friends. I have been very fortunate to have met and known other such warriors in my lifetime.

I don't know how it happened, but I know it has enriched my life in many ways and has given me the opportunity to work on projects over the years and support some of these men and their missions.

This book, my first attempt at writing, was meant to accomplish two things.

One, to entertain the reader for a few hours with what I hope you find to be a good story. And two, and most importantly, to pay tribute to and acknowledge some of the men I have known and others like them.

These men are seen and revered by the public for what they have done: the elite Special Operations Warriors. The legendary men capable of doing things the rest of us could never imagine.

But they are men—human. They have families: moms, dads, wives, and children. I wanted to bring a bit of humanity to who they are, even normalcy.

These men are larger than life. They are extraordinary for their sacrifice.

I look up to these men, not so much because they are Navy SEALs, Green Berets, etc., but rather for who they are as people, their character as individuals.

I hope I have done right by their character and to the reader.

Acknowledgements

I want to acknowledge those who have impacted me and my ability to write this book.

My wife, Susi, for her love and support.

My parents, Nita and Nolan, for their encouragement and support.

My friend Ron Relf, for his contributions to our country in many ways over the years and for being an inspiration. Thank you for your friendship.

Changiz Lahidji, the Chinese-Mexican. Also, for your friendship and for being a great American. Your commitment to this, your adopted nation, owes you a debt, and I hope your story is found by many and told countless times over.

To Terry "Doc" Weaver: writer, actor, director, and all-around superman. Thank you for being a friend. You have always said, "Everyone has a story to tell." Thank you for encouraging me to finish telling this one.

Dedications

This book is dedicated to the following:

To the friends we have lost along the way. May you forever be remembered.

To the Thin Blue Line: thank you for the thankless service you provide every day to serve and protect.

To the Thin Blue Line M.C. KSU & RYSD!

And finally, to the men and women in uniform; those brave few willing to put on the uniform and serve a higher calling.

Chapter 1

Avni Shala stood at the counter in his dark suit, smiling as he greeted and assisted guests checking in and out.

He was a pleasant, twenty-two-year-old man with dark hair, dark eyes, and a slim build, standing five feet eight inches tall. The hotel suit issued to him as part of the hotel's dress code policy hung loosely on his thin frame, as if it belonged to an older sibling.

Avni worked as an assistant desk clerk at the Le Méridien Grand Hotel in the Nuremberg Mitte district. It was a beautiful area of the city, popular with residents and tourists alike. The hotel was situated in the old town historical district, next to the central Bohnhoff train station.

He grew up in Pristina, Kosovo, in rather impoverished conditions, where he attended school. He learned German from his teachers and English from the local Americans.

Avni excelled in language classes and practiced with members of his mosque who also spoke English, as they worked for the Americans occupying that part of his country.

The Americans had been in Kosovo since being deployed in nineteen ninety-nine to help save the Albanians from the genocide taking place at the hands of the Serbian police and paramilitary groups, supported by then-Serbian President Slobodan Milosevic.

Money was tight for everyone in the region due to a lack of economic means and exports. The people struggled to make a living.

Under the occupation of the United States, money poured into Kosovo under the guise of helping the Albanian and Kosovo Muslims.

In fact, it inadvertently helped to open mosques that promoted 'Wahhabism,' which many around the world, including Muslims, believed to be a dangerous sect of the faith.

"Wahhabism" was Saudi Arabia's dominant sect of Islam, insisting on a literal interpretation of the Quran.

Wahhabis believed that if you did not practice their form of Islam, you were a heathen and an enemy of the faithful. For Christians, it would be akin to someone literally interpreting "an eye for an eye," or worse.

Avni had attended such a mosque in Pristina, just yards away from a statue of President Bill Clinton, who was President of the United States when the Americans came to Kosovo.

The religious teachers at the mosque instructed Avni to hate Americans as infidels and non-believers. He was taught that they were partially to blame for the economic depression and starvation of his people. Likewise, he was also taught that the Christians in Europe were to blame and needed to be dealt with according to the strict guidelines of the Quran.

That was how Avni came to be in Nuremberg.

The Imam from his mosque had recruited Avni to go to Europe, specifically Germany, to be of use to the Prophet as directed.

In the past few years, the Crown Prince of Saudi Arabia has made changes within the orthodoxy of the faith. Many in Avni's sect believed this to be cowardly, claiming the Crown Prince was bending to the will of the West, the non-believer. However, many others around the world believed that if they did not change their approach to the faith, they would end up on the wrong side of Orthodoxy and may perish in the afterlife.

The Imam who mentored Avni and a select group of other young men from the mosque in Pristina assured them that the faithful must mask their true intentions to fulfill the will of Allah. He assured them the Crown Prince was only placating the West to allow them to lower their defenses and enable the faithful to prevail.

Yesterday, Avni received a call on his mobile, giving him instructions to look for the name of a guest and report the guest's room number and check-in and check-out dates through his contact at the local Islamic center.

Due to the concerted efforts of the Germans in 2014 and the raids on mosques, apartments, and other places for what were called radical Islamists, extra precautions had to be taken when meeting or passing information, especially in planning attacks on non-believers. In the meantime, he had to smile and act pleasantly so the unfaithful would feel safe and comfortable around him.

John Spencer was the name of the guest Avni had been given. He was scheduled to check in tomorrow and would stay for the week in Room #560, which offered large accommodations and was nicely arranged. Clearly, this man was wealthy enough to afford such luxury. Whatever the reason his people wanted this man, Avni was sure he was guilty and deserved the penalty they would give him.

~~~

Sparse was an understatement.

The room was small compared to a standard American hotel room.

A full-sized platform-style bed with a European-style mattress and duvet occupied the space. The bed was clean but obviously showed years of use. A small side table with a lamp and a single bulb accompanied an older brown two-door wardrobe with no hangers and a chair in the corner. Soft spots in the underlying wooden floor, concealed by the worn seventies-era carpet, creaked underfoot.

The entire room measured about eight feet square. The door did not even open fully, pushing against the side of the bed three-quarters of the way before stopping. Small, but not surprising, even by German standards.

None of this was new to the man standing in the room.

Standing six feet tall, with black hair that appeared lighter due to the gray strands blending through, he had bright blue eyes that seemed to emit their own light. He was a solidly built man, showing years of conditioning and training, despite the few extra pounds he had gained around his waist in recent years.

Thirty years prior, his military career included multiple rotations to Panzer Kaserne near Stuttgart, in southwest Germany, with the 1st Battalion, 10th Special Forces, and the Mobile Training Team (MTT).
~~~

He honestly looked forward to those breaks from deployments in Lebanon, Somalia, Nigeria, Rwanda, Kosovo, and other places he preferred to keep in the past.

John Spencer had been an NCO (Non-Commissioned Officer) in "The Teams," going through the Q-Course and selection right out of PLDC (Primary Leadership Development Course).

A prerequisite, PLDC was a military course that trained junior enlisted personnel to think and lead based on the strong leadership qualities and thought processes the Army required NCOs to maintain in order to keep the "troops" in line and alive in battle. Mostly, what Spencer remembered from PLDC was a repeat of Basic Training, where senior NCOs tossed your rack and clothes for not being rolled to the exact size and width of a dollar bill. It was mostly a month-long period of basics that one couldn't fail unless they had the IQ of a cucumber.

Two months after completing PLDC, he was temporarily assigned to Special Forces Preparation and Conditioning.

Once completed to standard, he moved on to the initial Qualification and Selection, Phase One, of the training program at Ft. Bragg, where he was processed and transported to Camp Mackall to begin the 24-day training cycle.

It was a fifty-six-week, physically and mentally grueling assault on everything one thought they or their body could endure; then, they turned things up a notch from there.

Spencer grew up in an abusive home as a child in Texas.

His father was a sad and abusive man who blamed others for his own failures in life and thus drank excessively. When he did, he became physically abusive.

Donald Spencer was a high school dropout with no fallback plan. He was a tall man who appeared much smaller than he was due to his personality and attitude. Thinning hair, a perpetual stubble that matched his disheveled appearance, and bad breath characterized him.

The man had no training or skills; he couldn't hold a job and, even worse, couldn't hold his tongue. He had been fired from one job after another for mouthing off to his boss. On more than one occasion, he paid for it with an ass-kicking. Those were the worst days.

Don Spencer would come home drunk and hit Spencer's mother, Marcia—a kindhearted, mousy, and demure woman who did as she was told. She spoke little and accepted her fate as penance for having a roof over her head.

The Elder Spencer didn't just beat Marcia; John would hear the abuse from behind closed doors as a kid: his mother screaming into a pillow and whimpering afterward for what seemed like forever until Don would come out of the bedroom, walk to the refrigerator in his boxers, and grab a beer. Spencer was too young to understand at the time that his mother was being raped and sexually abused by his father.

At thirteen, Spencer came home from school on a Wednesday afternoon to find his mother gone. The small shack of a house they lived in was trashed. The furniture had been knocked over, and the dishes were broken. There, passed out drunk on the sofa, was the culprit, Don Spencer.

John found a note under his pillow that night from his mother.

"I'm sorry, Johnny,

please forgive me.

I love you,

Mom."

The note was bittersweet. He was sad he no longer had his mother, but he was happy she had escaped the brutality of his father. At least she would be better off somewhere else—anywhere else but there.

The next four years were excruciating for John. He stayed up late studying every night, determined to graduate early and get away from Don Spencer as soon as possible.

He woke up early and went to the high school gym to work out with the football and wrestling teams. Running relays, lifting weights, calisthenics, etc., he would strengthen himself to make the beatings hurt less, at least physically.

John never joined the sports teams at school. He had never wanted to be a part of a team; at this point in his life, everyone he knew had let him down. He needed to be his own team, stand up for himself, and make sure no one else could ever hurt him or take advantage of him again.

In his senior year of high school, an Army recruiter came to career day at his school. The recruiter's name was Staff Sergeant Wilkins. He was a large, imposing man, about six feet five inches tall. His uniform fit like a well-pressed suit of armor. SSG Wilkins looked like he could pick up the back end of a Chrysler and still have strength left over.

John listened to what the recruiter had to say about "Honor and Integrity," learning a career, money for college, and traveling the world—all of which checked the boxes of what John Spencer wanted and had been working for in his own life.

That day, John went home after school to a drunken Don Spencer, who was angry as hell at the dumb son of a bitch who had fired him. When John attempted to go to his room, his father yelled at him.

"Don't turn your back on me, you worthless little shit!"

Don grabbed John by the shoulder to turn him around. At that moment, reacting on instinct, John drew back and knocked Don Spencer on his ass with one blow.

Don lay there on the floor, bleeding and a little disoriented, not sure of what had just happened. John leaned over his father and grabbed him by the shirt.

"If you ever lay another hand on me, I promise it will be the last time you touch anyone or anything ever again."

Two months later, John Spencer graduated from high school. He didn't bother attending his graduation, opting instead to go straight to the recruiting station and enlist. John decided he wanted to help people who couldn't help themselves, and the only thing he could think of was becoming a combat medic.

Six weeks later, Private John Spencer was on his way to Fort Jackson, S.C., for Basic Training.

But that was a long, long time ago and thousands of miles away.

Spencer's life had changed several times since then: Special Forces selection, marriage, fifteen years in the Army, divorce, early retirement, and a few years of special assignments with the CIA. Those were interesting assignments indeed, and most of them were still classified. Then there was a stint back home in Houston, where he served on the SWAT team as an active member and training instructor.

Yes, a lot of things had changed since those days in high school, when he hadn't aspired to be part of a team. He learned quickly as part of the "ODA" (Operational Detachment Alpha, or "A-Teams," as they were more commonly known). You don't get far on your own, and there is no "I" in team.

The team had his back more than the family he was born into ever did. They taught him how to trust, at least from a team perspective; it turned out to be the most difficult part of training for him. But the teams changed his life and his outlook. And oddly enough, the unpredictable and extraordinary life of Special Forces helped him learn to be… well, normal in a way.

Spencer was in Nuremberg because of a promise he made to himself upon retiring from his last job as head of security for Bedford Offshore Drilling Services.

Bedford was an offshore exploration company that owned and operated nearly fifty oil rigs and drill ships around the world.

Spencer had been shot in the line of duty rescuing a woman during a hostage situation in downtown Houston. The perpetrator was a career criminal who had tried to rob a bank. After the shooting, he received a call from an old Agency contact who had a lead for him.

The company was expanding its global operations into some shady parts of the world, like Egypt, Angola, Nigeria, and Libya. The company needed someone with a proper understanding of those locations—someone who had contacts in those areas and could read geopolitical situations and make informed decisions on personnel deployments and risk assessments.

The pay was a pleasant change from government salaries, and the benefits were nothing to sneeze at either. A simple job sitting behind a desk, for the most part, and reviewing global assessments daily. He could afford the retirement he had hoped for.

So, he promised himself that after he retired for good, he would travel the world and see the places he had not had the luxury or time to enjoy before, and do it at a leisurely pace on his own schedule. Which is why he was sitting in this square box of a guesthouse in Nuremberg.

His reservations at the Le Méridien had gotten mixed up, or so the hotel manager had told him. All the rooms in the city were fully booked for the Climate Conference that was currently being held. The only accommodation he could find was a room at Frau Knopf's Gasthaus, south of the Old Town.

Spencer booked the room and would make the most of his few days here in Nuremberg. He would attempt to correct his booking tomorrow. For now, he was jet lagged from the flight in from Houston. But since it was still fairly early in the day and he was hungry, he made his way to the old town city center, where rumor had it there was an old-fashioned restaurant that served roasted pig shoulders and the best unfiltered Weißbier in the city.

Dressed in a pair of Mott & Bow jeans, Johnston and Murphy Upton knit loafers, and a casual button-down shirt with a Brooks Brothers V-neck sweater, Spencer looked more like a European executive than a former operator.

Chapter 2

The plans had changed. Avni had now been instructed to go to the Afghan protest in Nuremberg's Old Town Square. The protest was being conducted by a local group of Afghan Muslims who were protesting the Taliban and Al-Qaeda in their country. Avni had never been to the Middle East, and he didn't really relish the idea. Aside from Hajj, the annual pilgrimage to Saudi Arabia that all faithful of the Prophet Muhammad should make at least once during their lives, he had no desire to go, especially to Afghanistan.

His life before coming to Germany had been cold and hungry, with little to no prospects for jobs. Unless he left his home, there was not much chance of happiness or joy that he could hope for. And he knew, after years of lessons at the mosque, that his reward was not to be here on this earth. His suffering and faithfulness would be rewarded in heaven.

Not that he was in a rush to get to heaven, but he knew it would be worth it when it happened. For now, he was content with his small apartment that he shared with another hotel employee. His apartment wasn't luxurious, but it was clean and warm—more than he had as a child. And he had food to eat. He ate at the hotel for free on the days he worked, which was six days a week, and he had food in the refrigerator in his apartment for when he was hungry. Things most Europeans and Americans took for granted, but not Avni. He knew the feeling of hunger and despair, and he did not take it for granted. The Imam had given him an opportunity to come here and helped pay his expenses until he could get this job, as the Imam had wanted. Avni was prepared to repay the kindness whenever asked and in whatever way expected. He had no desire to die, but if asked, he was ready and would receive his reward.

Avni had been told to meet his contact at the protest in front of the Frauenkirche in Old Town, close to the hotel where he worked. This would raise less suspicion, as both of them would blend in with those in attendance. The Frauenkirche, which means "Church of Our Lady," was a Catholic church dating back to the mid-twelfth century. The idea of a religious house of worship honoring a woman went against the teachings he knew and understood.

Avni only knew his contact by the name of Samir. Samir was from Slovenia, and he and Avni prayed together at the mosque. They did not socialize for fear of being identified by the authorities, something the Imam had been very clear about when giving Avni his instructions before leaving Pristina. He was to be social at work, even with non-believers, so as not to raise suspicion. He was to attend the local mosque for prayers and remain faithful to his purpose. Avni obeyed the Imam's instructions. He did not socialize outside of work. He had to be careful not to let the influence of these heathens infect him.

There had been a few times, while politely taking part in conversations with other employees about soccer or other such frivolous topics, that he found himself smiling or laughing. Not that this wasn't part of his cover to be pleasant, but at those moments, he caught himself feeling happy and friendly with these people. Avni was ashamed of this afterward. He had let his guard down and allowed their influence to affect him. He would have to pay closer attention not to fall prey to such weakness.

The task was simple: stand by the large bench areas in front of the church, but not too close; Samir would find him. Once Avni was standing next to Samir, he would do his best to pass the details on John Spencer to him without being noticed.

~~~

The weather was a very pleasant seventy-three degrees as he walked along Plobenhofstrasse. Spencer was enjoying his leisurely stroll through the Old Town square and the beautiful old-world architecture that Europeans had maintained and incorporated into the modern world.
~~~

There was a stark contrast between the fourteenth-century buildings and the twenty-first-century coffee shops that lined the perimeter of the square. Of course, the entrance to the old town square, made of sandstone block walls built in the thirteenth century, still featured old-fashioned buildings and businesses that catered to the tourists who came to shop at the Christmas market and immerse themselves in a time long since passed.

This was a pleasant change of pace and unusual for Spencer to be so relaxed and not thinking about work, the potential risks of global operations, or the plethora of other thoughts that had been part of his daily life for so many years. Retirement had thus far been bittersweet, and he was learning to let go and relax.

He was so absorbed in enjoying the sights of the old city architecture —made up of buildings and features from the Middle Ages and Renaissance periods, with influences from the late Gothic and Baroque eras—that he failed to notice the sounds of a protest until he was around the corner from it. He was walking past the gelato stand at the corner of Plobenhofstrasse and Hauptmarkt Square when he finally noticed the loud voices coming over a speaker or bullhorn and a crowd chanting in Arabic, which sounded like Pashto.

As Spencer drew closer, he could see what appeared to be a large group of people protesting. Based on the language and ethnic appearance, he assumed they were Muslim immigrants or refugees. He made this assumption based on what many of the people were wearing.

The men wore traditional white-colored Paran tops and tumban trousers of the same color, while the locals wore more Western-styled clothes, such as jeans and T-shirts. They were all gathered in a crowd in front of the Frauenkirche, a beautiful piece of Gothic religious architecture built in the mid-thirteen hundreds by the Holy Roman Emperor, Charles IV. Spencer knew this from his research of the area online when determining what he wanted to see while he was in town.

Spencer's hypervigilant nature took over, and he automatically began scanning and assessing the situation and the crowd simultaneously.

From his experience in the Middle East and abroad in Europe, he knew these types of events had been used to mask more sinister intentions, like suicide bombers or IEDs. What he quickly determined here were peaceful crowds respectfully protesting the Taliban in Afghanistan and pleading with Germany and the United States to help those trapped in their country and protect the innocent people still living there.

Muslim women without hijabs and Muslim men in Western clothes gathered together in peaceful protest. These were young Muslims who had fled the bloodshed in their countries and assimilated into the Western culture of their adoptive nations. This generation wanted peace and freedom from the religious persecution that had killed so many of their friends and family.

Someone handed Spencer a flyer printed in both German and English, which translated what was being said.

"Please, *your* help *to* save Afghan people from the Taliban. Thank you, America, and Germany."

At least the grammar was better than that of some American public schools these days.

Spencer was aware of the multitudes of immigrants from all over the Middle East who had made their way into Germany and other European countries because Angela Merkel had opened the floodgates to the EU without consulting its citizens or the European people about their views.

Merkel had faced political backlash ever since, yet somehow continued to survive re-election for years, until recently.

Female German citizens had been sexually harassed and assaulted since the mass migrations started, and the number of "honor killings" had risen exponentially. Likewise, male citizens in Europe were finding themselves attacked or killed by knife-wielding lunatics who opposed the Western lifestyle: the clothes they wore, the food they ate, and people holding hands or kissing in public.

Yes, there were many incidents of European men being chased and killed by machete-wielding Muslim men who were ranting and lashing out against those who had accepted and taken them in. All because they expected everyone to follow their way of life and religion.

The crowd of people Spencer was observing seemed to be respectful individuals who were concerned for their homeland and begging for help. Based on the current administrations on both sides of the Atlantic, it didn't seem that help was likely to come any time soon.

In fact, the administration of the United States at the time had bungled the entire withdrawal.

They had made such a mess of the pullout from Afghanistan that they had inadvertently left the Taliban billions of dollars worth of military equipment. Not only that, but they also left hundreds of Americans to be used as hostages—or worse.

At that moment, the Taliban were hunting them down to kill those who had helped and aided the Americans for twenty years.

The American public was outraged at the chaotic way the pullout had been handled.

Veterans and active-duty military members felt angry, believing their sacrifices, and those of their brothers and sisters who never made it home, were all for nothing.

No matter how one looked at it, from a political point of view or the military front, it was yet another government FUBAR caused by inept politicians rather than military leaders on the ground who better understood the complexities of war.

Many believed this war would have to be fought again at some point down the road.

Spencer felt for the Afghan people. He had worked alongside some of the younger Afghan men who served as combat interpreters on a couple of his missions with the Agency during the hunt for Abu-Sul Malik, or the Amir, as he had become known—a terrorist mastermind that the U.S. and its allies had been hunting for his attacks on American and European citizens around the world and who was at the time a central leader of Al-Qaeda.

Spencer, along with a couple of Special Forces operators on loan to the Agency and a couple of Afghan "Terps," short for interpreters, were scouting some of the mountainous terrain along the border in response to reports of sightings of the Amir in a mission codenamed "Grass Hopper," because the Amir was always jumping from one place to another, making it hard to track his whereabouts.

One of the team members was originally from Iran and spoke perfect Arabic. His Pashto wasn't very good, but he could get by.

Since Spencer and the other team members couldn't speak Arabic or Pashto, the plan was to use the two combat interpreters to act as guides for the three Americans, posing as mentally incapacitated tribal members.

They would essentially be playing deaf, dumb, and blind—minus the blind part.

This was only if they encountered a group of Al-Qaeda or the Taliban who got too close or started asking questions. It was an audacious plan, but the only one they could devise that didn't involve disclosing they were American, or at least Westerners.

Even though they were in the middle of extremely rugged and dangerous mountain terrain, it wasn't beyond the realm of possibility to run into bad guys hiding up there.

After about a day and a half of hiking through the Tora Bora mountains, they spotted a group of men along the edge of a mountain with a large cave entrance and a well-worn dirt and rock path leading up the embankment to a flattened area in front of the cave's entrance.

Assured that they had not been spotted by the men, the team regrouped and went over their plan. This was a risk, and the team knew it; they all accepted it. They weren't sure about risking their lives on the idea of acting like Jim Carrey and Jeff Daniels in Dumb and Dumber, but it was all they had at the moment, and time was running out. They agreed, and the team began making its way up the embankment.

"Abbasi," a master sergeant in the ODA originally from Tehran, was a bit of a prankster. Since no one could tell by just looking at him if he was Asian or Latino, he would joke that he was the "Asian-Taco" of the group.

At five feet eleven inches tall, with bushy, salt-and-pepper hair that was about four months overdue for a cut and a semi-long goatee, Abbasi fit right in once he covered his head. Since they were all wearing the traditional clothing of the local Afghans, their attire did not give them away.

The other team member was a Staff Sergeant named "Morris."

He was of Asian and Russian descent and fit in appearance-wise because of the number of Russian and Afghan blends in the country, remnants of when Russian troops invaded and pillaged the locals during their occupation in the nineteen eighties.

Oddly enough, this was also the time when the United States was helping fund, train, and arm the Mujahideen through the Pakistan Security Service, ultimately funding the Amir in his efforts to force the Russians out of Afghanistan.

But that was an onion to be peeled another day. The mission they were on at the moment was to investigate reports of the Amir's whereabouts and report back.

Their interpreters were two young Afghan men named "Z" and "Slim." The American teams they had worked with gave Z that nickname because his real name was impossible for Americans to pronounce, and Slim earned his name because he was so skinny he looked like a tall pencil. Both men were in their mid-twenties and determined to eliminate Al-Qaeda and the Taliban.

The boys knew they were risking their lives to help the Americans and were more than happy to do so if it meant bringing change to their country. Spencer had a lot of respect for those two men. It reminded him of America's history and the fight for independence, and the patriots who would risk everything for the experiment that was democracy.

Honestly, that day they all earned an Oscar for their performances.

The three Americans had to act mentally deficient. Z and Slim were guiding them up the path while pretending to be unaware of the men above them.

Suddenly, a group of men armed with AK-47s rounded the corner of the path, pointing their weapons at the team of five. The Afghans waved their rifles in the team's direction as they yelled at them.

The three Americans had service-issued handguns and additional rounds hidden under their loose-fitting Peran tops, but they were not easily accessible. They were outnumbered now, and if they needed to draw their weapons, they would not make it out alive.

'Z' and 'Slim,' referred to as 'the boys,' looked up, startled, and started apologizing to the men on the path, who were apparently asking questions as 'Z' kept motioning with his arms toward the three Americans in disguise. The three of them just stood there, oblivious to what was going on around them, trying their best to monitor the men on the cliff face above through their peripheral vision.

One of the Afghan men on the worn dirt path started making his way toward the group, while the other two men accompanying him stood their ground. All three men kept their rifles pointed in the team's direction. The man who approached the group looked at each of them. First at Z, then at Slim, and finally at the three Americans, who were huddled together.

The Afghan man started speaking to the three Americans. Spencer and Morris did not understand what the man was saying, but Abbasi grasped some of it; he didn't respond. When the three operatives didn't answer, the suspected Taliban man began yelling at them.

Slim tried to intervene and say something, but the man hit him in the gut with the butt of his rifle.

Abbasi, playing his role well, began mumbling in an agitated state, making more noise than coherent words. Morris and Spencer mimicked Abbasi's actions, shifting their weight from one foot to the other in a rocking motion, as if terribly upset.

The scene was a little chaotic but believable because the goat-smelling man who had hit Slim was now yelling at Slim and Z, motioning with his arm and hand for them to go away. The boys agreed and took the three childlike Americans by the arms, turning them around.

As Spencer was turning, he leaned back to get a good look at the cliff face and saw that men had gathered to watch the commotion. Right in the middle of about eight men overlooking the path was Abu-Sul Malik, "The Amir."

The mission had been a success, or at least Spencer thought so. The team double-timed their way back to Jalalabad, where they met the station chief for a debrief.

The men detailed their findings and Spencer's positive visual of Abu-Sul Malik, as well as the GPS coordinates of where the terrorists were hiding. Once the team was debriefed, the three men, including their interpreters, went their separate ways.

In his multiple follow-ups over the next several weeks, Spencer learned the Agency had not, in fact, followed up on the visual of the Amir and would not be doing so. Directly, he had been told that the war was too important and there was too much riding on its continuation at the time to be cut short by taking out the number one target on their list.

Whether that meant they would be pulled out before completing other necessary operations against other terrorist operatives, or whether, more akin to a "too big to fail" mindset regarding government contractors, Spencer would never know. He was disgusted. Disgusted with the Agency, with the military, and with the mindset of how war was being fought these days.

He was put on a Black Hawk helicopter and sent to Bagram Air Base for a flight back to Langley an hour after being told to back off. At that moment, Spencer realized he was just a cog in the wheel and nothing more. No longer the dangerous tip of the spear, he was now an expendable intelligence gatherer sent on risky missions to gather intel that served no apparent purpose. What was worse, it risked the lives of two warriors of conscience and two young men willing to risk their lives for what they believed would help their own country.

That was Spencer's last rotation with the Agency.

Abu-Sul Malik died in a raid by SEAL Team Six two years later in a compound on the border of Pakistan and Afghanistan.

Now, a world away and years later, in the safe, beautiful old town square of Nuremberg, Germany, Spencer faced the reality of the old saying, "The more things change, the more they stay the same."

The country of Afghanistan was once again in the grips of the Taliban and Al-Qaeda, and these people were begging for help from the countries that were supposed to have provided it twenty years earlier.

Spencer shook his head in shame, wishing them well and maybe offering a bit of a prayer that somehow the plight of these people would be lessened and that better days were ahead, but he doubted it.

Then, he turned and started walking back toward the Gasthaus. Suddenly, he wasn't so hungry.

~~~

Attractive by anyone's standards, with long, shapely legs, dark hair that fell just below her shoulders, and a very fit and firm body that made men take notice.

From Sarajevo, Emina Begić was fifteen years old in the summer of 1992 when the Serbs surrounded the capital and began shooting at citizens and bombing her city.
~~~

Artillery, tanks, heavy machine guns, and rocket launchers were set up in the hills surrounding the capital city.

Snipers were positioned throughout the area and would take out anyone they thought was a threat or for target practice if they were bored.

Women had been raped and murdered by these sinister monsters. The wretched and insidious assault the Serbs committed on her people, those called 'Bosniaks,' was beyond 'atrocities,' as they had been labeled during Milosevic's trial.

Emina's father had been beaten in the street for sport and then shot in the head, even though he lay there, defeated and refusing to fight back. The Serbian soldiers walked away, laughing afterward. He had been a good man and a kind father. He would take her and her mother on vacation during the summer to Lake Modrac, where they would swim, play, and have picnics together.

Her mother was killed later when a mortar round struck the building she was in while helping to take care of an elderly neighbor woman who was sick and unable to care for herself.

Emina had grown angry and carried that anger deep in her heart. As she grew older, she wanted revenge and sought ways to get even with the men who had played a part in the deaths of her family and those in her community.

The determined woman found groups of men who planned such missions to seek justice for these atrocious acts. The angry girl inside her volunteered to help them. They would plan attacks at restaurants, gas stations, parks—wherever the opportunity presented itself.

The group eventually used explosives to ensure the destruction of the men and their homes, just as they had done to hers, making a statement to others that this is what you get for such evil acts. Muslims had been attacked and mistreated for long enough.

She wasn't devout; she didn't wear a hijab or go to a mosque, but she was Muslim, and her people had been targeted for that reason. Emina spent twenty-five years making them, and people like them, pay. Now in her forties, she knew nothing else.

The woman terrorist had been instructed to apply for a job at the Le Méridien Hotel in Nuremberg a month ago. She didn't know why, but she didn't ask questions either.

The female operative assumed there was a plan, and she would know soon enough what it was.

She had been given a false identity under the name “Lena Markovich” from Pristina. The thought of posing as a Serbian, even for the cause, made her sick to her stomach, but she did as she was told.

She had received a knock at her door the night before her task. A man in his twenties, maybe older, stood in the doorway. Tall, almost six feet, slender but well-built. Attractive and most likely Eastern European, perhaps of Slavic descent. He was dressed in slacks and a casual-style jacket, holding a backpack. He glanced at her briefly, then handed her the backpack. No words were exchanged. She took the backpack, and then the man turned and walked away.

Emina closed and locked her apartment door and walked to the kitchen, where she placed the backpack on a small kitchen table and unzipped it.

Inside were the tools she had used many times before: Semtex, a detonator, and a sensor device similar to those used on windows for home security. Once the current to the sensor is broken, the device is activated.

There, inside the bag, was also a piece of paper on which was written “RM #560.”

Chapter 3

Apparently, jet lag got worse the older you got, thought Spencer. It was nine in the morning, and he was just waking up. He had walked back to his room from the Old Town yesterday, which turned out to be a little farther than he expected—about six miles overall.

In the old days, he could have done that after a night out drinking with no problem, he thought. Now, at fifty-six, having sat behind a desk for the past ten years before retiring, he wasn't as fit as he once had been. Sitting for ten hours a day, plus better money and better restaurants, had a way of widening the midsection and lowering motivation for high performance day in and day out. Or, at least, that was the impact it had on him.

Halfway between Old Town and the Gasthaus, Spencer stopped at a gyro stand to quell the grumbling in his stomach, which temporarily curbed the rumbling. He had been up and down all night from jet lag and the gyro, which was why he slept until nine a.m. this morning.

Twenty minutes later, he was downstairs in the common dining room, where Frau Knopf had kept some breakfast for him: some Brötchen (German bread), cheese, butter, and a soft-boiled egg. Frau Knopf, realizing he was American, had also made him a carafe of café Americano.

Spencer thought it was women like her who kept men going.

Frau Knopf came back to the table and handed him a small envelope and, in her German accent, said, "This message come for you."

At first, Spencer was confused, as no one knew he was even in Germany, let alone at Frau Knopf's Gasthaus.

"I'm sorry, I think you have the wrong guest."

"Nein, the man said Amerikan, you are only Amerikan here," she replied.

As Frau Knopf walked away, Spencer looked down at the white envelope and turned it over. On the front, written by hand, were the words "Grasshopper Taco."

Spencer knew immediately who the message was from. But how he knew Spencer was here was another question altogether, as was why he was receiving the message at all.

Spencer opened the envelope and read:

"Zum Spiessgesellen 2 p.m."

This was the restaurant Spencer had planned to eat at yesterday before being confronted with a memory that, coincidentally, involved the same person he was about to meet at 2 p.m.

"Behnam Abbasi."

Spencer wasn't much of a believer in coincidence. Somehow, he knew that the events from yesterday were tied to his receiving this message from Abbasi, nearly a decade after working with him on the mission in Tora Bora. But why?

~~~

Behnam Abbasi was from Shapoor, Iran.

He grew up in a time and place much different from what it is known to the rest of the world today. Growing up in Iran was a fun experience for Abbasi. There was no Ayatollah, no caliphate, or jihad in those days.

The Shah ruled Iran. Those were peaceful times. Men did not wear the traditional Qameh shirts or Jubba pants they do today, and women were not forced to wear hijabs to cover themselves. In fact, women could vote, study at the university, and drive cars.

Behnam's mother drove a pale yellow, convertible 1965 Ford Mustang with tufted bucket seats. It had been his favorite American car.

Behnam's father had been the mayor of the town they lived in, and his parents were very social people. His father and mother would throw parties for their friends. During the hot summers, they would sleep on mattresses on the roof for what little breeze they could get.
~~~

Behnam's parents followed the prophet Zoroaster, raising him with the belief that truth was the only way to wisdom. The main tenets of Zarathustra were 'Good thoughts, Good words, and Good deeds.'

Abbasi had been enthralled with the United States since he was a boy. He went to the movies every chance he had.

One day in early nineteen sixty-nine, Abbasi went to see a new John Wayne film called "The Green Berets." That was the day that changed his life forever. From that moment on, he knew without a doubt that he wanted to be a Green Beret.

Behnam's uncle "Mo" had migrated to the United States twenty years earlier and started a chain of hamburger restaurants in the Midwest. So, his father arranged for Behnam to go to the United States to live with his uncle and finish school. Behnam excelled in all his classes. He ran track and worked summers on local farms, bailing hay and doing other jobs to help build his muscle and endurance.

The day he graduated, he went straight to the recruiting office and joined the Army. He told the recruiter he aspired to be a Green Beret.

The recruiter had laughed, half at Behnam's accent and the other half because he didn't think the kid could make it. But the recruiter signed him up for 18F: Special Forces candidate, anyway.

Abbasi was on his way to the qualification training, referred to as the "Q" Course, at the JFK Special Warfare Center and School at Fort Bragg, North Carolina.

Almost two years later, Behnam Abbasi graduated as a Green Beret combat medic and was assigned to his first unit: Fifth Special Forces Group.

After twenty-seven years in the teams, he had retired. Benham had been involved in almost every military conflict since Vietnam. He decided it was time to trade in the OD green uniform and take a job with the CIA. They had been offering him a position for a few years, and he had continued to put it off. He had loved serving in the special forces, serving his adoptive country that had given him so much. But he felt it was time to serve in a different capacity.

Now, after a lengthy Army career and several years with the agency, he was tired. He was ready to settle back and enjoy life, whatever that meant. Maybe he would visit family, maybe try fishing, or maybe he would just sit back and watch the old movies on TV that he had loved as a kid.

Benham Abbasi had volunteered for this assignment. He had been part of Operation Grasshopper, where the men were being targeted. He thought highly of John Spencer, recalling how he conducted himself during the operation in Tora Bora. He wanted to take part in this mission. It was personal. But he decided this would be the last one. After this, he was finished.

~~~

At 1:48 p.m., Spencer was walking up the stairs to Zu Spiessgesellen, a fairly open and large place with many tables and sections divided by uneven, rustic-looking walls. The restaurant was painted white to give it an old-world appeal, reminiscent of what it may have looked like a hundred years ago or more.

Spencer could smell the pork roasting on a mechanical spit along the wall. The establishment had few patrons, as the lunch crowd had left by this time of day. It didn't take Spencer long to spot the man he was looking for. Sitting in a small section to the right of the main bar area, at a corner table against the window and angled so that both seats had a view of the restaurant, wearing a tan trench coat, was Behnam Abbasi.

He was a little grayer in his hair than Spencer remembered, and he was without the beard. A pleasant-looking man who appeared unimposing and docile, but someone Spencer knew could be as deadly as he himself once was.

Spencer calmly walked to the table where Abbasi stood to greet him. The two men took a moment to assess one another, then exchanged the quick and strong embrace that brothers and warriors share in respect and admiration.

He waited for Abbasi to make the first comment.

"Spencer, it's been a long time. How have you been?" Abbasi asked, in what seemed like an honest and curious question. But Spencer understood this game all too well.

"Considering you knew how and where to find me, I assume you know exactly how I am. I'm guessing you're with the Agency now?" Spencer responded without a hint of animus in his voice.
~~~

"Spencer, nothing dubious meant at all. In fact, quite the opposite. And yes, I went through The Farm a couple of months after you left."

"I assume you have been tracking me since before I got here?"

"Correct. I started following up on you two weeks before you left for vacation. Sorry about your reservations at the Le Méridien; I know they would have been nicer accommodations."

"You're the reason my reservations were canceled?"

"Guilty. And for a good reason. Actually, they weren't canceled. I arranged for the hotel staff to keep the room in your name but tell you that it had been canceled, and that the hotel was fully booked."

"Well, Frau Knopf is happy, I'm sure, but I can't say that I am."

"The Amir," Abbasi said, cutting Spencer off mid-sentence.

That moniker brought an immediate, albeit momentary, silence to the conversation.

"What about him? He's been dead for over seven years," Spencer finally responded.

Abbasi looked Spencer in the eyes without saying a word.

"You can't be serious? It's not possible," Spencer replied in aggravated disbelief.

"Six took him out themselves," he continued matter-of-factly, hoping this would settle the question at hand.

"It was a decoy. The man Six took out was a decoy, a lookalike. And a damn good one at that. Fingerprints were burned off so as not to identify the body, and the teeth were capped. They could never identify the body one hundred percent, and they never did DNA sampling."

"Jesus, when did you guys find this out?"

"About six months ago. Another agency operation discovered details on a laptop recovered during a small terrorist cell takedown. There was information that showed The Amir may actually be alive. We have been tracking leads for the past few months. A small but deadly new player in the 'let's blow someone up' stage is thought to be the work of 'The Amir.'

"What group?" Spencer inquired.

"Shahid–TB," was the spook's answer.

Spencer was aware of some of the activities of the new group. "Shahid" translated to "Martyr." "Shahid-TB" literally meant "Martyr–Tora Bora." If true, and if the Amir were still alive, it made sense.

They had no known base of operations, and they had been very specific in their targeting of international locations and people. Low-key, but with specific personnel who had been part of operations linked to finding The Amir in the past. Initially, it had been thought that the group had been started by a small faction of the Amir's loyalists that broke away from Al-Qaeda.

But if the Amir actually survived, this would make much more sense. The hard part was finding a group that had no geographic base of operations and one in which you didn't actually know who the players were. Many of the Amir's old guard had been captured and were now at Guantanamo Bay prison. America had a naval base of operations nearby. So there had to be new players and new loyalists.

"That sucks for Six and is a bit of a black eye for the Agency, since they never followed up on our mission debrief."

"The Amir knows about Operation Grasshopper," Abbasi said.

Spencer sat there and stared at Abbasi for what seemed like minutes. "What did you just say?"

"He knows about 'Grasshopper,' and we are assuming he knows who the people were that were involved. Slim was found dead, tortured and displayed in the center of his village so his tribe would get the message. We haven't found "Z" yet, but we assume the same.

We believe Shahid-TB was created as his personal jihad to get revenge on those who tracked him down, in an effort to take them out."

"But we didn't. The agency never followed up on the visual confirmation, and he changed locations and was never captured or killed as a result."

"True, but it doesn't mean he had all the facts, which is why I tracked you down. We believe he is out to kill anyone and everyone related to Operation Grasshopper. I wanted to reach out and brief you personally."

"What about Morris?" Spencer asked.

"He was shot during a team operation in Syria two years ago. He didn't make it."

Spencer bowed his head for a moment, remembering the warrior who had helped them years ago. Morris was a good man and a damn good warrior. Spencer told himself it was better to die a warrior's death than to be taken out by a cowardly terrorist or blindsided. "And the protests yesterday in front of the Frauenkirche? Is this a demonstration the Agency helped to orchestrate?"

"You can take the boy out of the farm, but you can't take the farm out of the boy."

"Cute; your Americanisms seem to have gotten better." Minor sarcasm was meant more to tease another former Team guy and not as an ethnic or immigrant insult. These types of quips were a common, if not expected, aspect of military life that one never fully let go of. In some strange way, it showed respect for one's brother-in-arms.

Abbasi gave a short but acknowledged chuckle.

"Yes, we have assisted with some funding and resources to help these immigrants print materials and draft their message without them knowing the agency was specifically involved. Mostly, money is provided through shell organizations funded by USAID.

The movement and desire are all legitimate to their cause. They remind me of guys like 'Z' and 'Slim' who truly cared about the future of their country. These people honestly want the Allies to help bring peace to Afghanistan and get rid of the Taliban and Al-Qaeda once and for all. They can't understand how, after two decades, nothing has really changed and now, we are negotiating with the people we were fighting and allowing them to take back control of the country while basically supplying them with billions of dollars in military equipment."

"Yeah, well, they're not the only ones," Spencer quipped.

The server came by to take their order, and they both ordered the roast pork shoulder and a Weissbier.

Abbasi was not a devout Muslim. He had made the decision not to follow all the tenets when he joined the Army and, ultimately, the Special Forces. Being a Muslim in the Special Forces, especially an Iranian during the Iran hostage situation, was not a pleasant experience.

Even before the hostage situation, he was viewed with suspicion and treated as a pariah. His own teammates would tell him to go back to where he had come from, making it very difficult for him to pursue a life dedicated to his adopted country.

Abbasi had seen firsthand what blind religious ideologies could do to people and decided, as a young adult, that he could maintain his beliefs without attaching all the limitations and restrictions to them. His will was stronger than their ignorance, and he prevailed. He chose to be an American first and foremost and wanted to fit in—not only to change his circumstances but also to change the mindset of those he trained and bled with, as well as their misconceptions toward other Muslims in the future. As a result, he learned he liked pork, especially pulled pork sandwiches and cold beer, though he still observed certain holidays for his family's sake.

Never married and with no kids, his family consisted of his mother, uncles, and sisters. He spent time with his nephews and nieces when he could.

However, the life he had chosen as an Operator in the Teams and now in the CIA left little time to pursue a family or a fulfilling home life. A sacrifice, he told himself, was worth his contribution to a country that had given him and his family a better life than the one they would have had if they had stayed in Iran.

But he never considered the life America owed him for everything he had done for it. For all the chest-beating he did as part of the teams in his younger days, Abbasi was a humble man. Indeed, the country did owe him a lot for his actions and dedication, but unfortunately, he could never be acknowledged for it—definitely not in the way he deserved.

During lunch, they made some occasional small talk.

Abbasi caught him up on how he was recruited into the agency after Operation Grasshopper, and Spencer filled him in on a few other details about his career after leaving the agency, much of which Abbasi was already aware.

The SWAT situation in Houston had garnered some national attention, and guys in the Special Operations community do talk and keep track of one another.

"Spencer, as the Field Case Officer on Grasshopper, we suspect you are a primary target of The Amir's attention. We are surprised he hasn't tried anything so far."

"Well, Homeland is pretty good at its job, and I haven't been outside the country until now for nearly five years."

"And that's why we are reaching out. You're in Europe on vacation —no backup, traveling alone, no weapons. You are at your most vulnerable, which is why we switched your hotel in case we were not the only ones tracking you. Any interest in working with us on this one, since you were the lead on Grasshopper and potentially a prime target at this point?"

"I've been out of the Agency for too many years—much longer than I was ever in. I can't say I look forward to the idea, no."

"I'm kind of surprised to hear you say that," said Abbasi. "We could reinstate you, even for a short period, and help provide you with some resources to keep you safe."

"Appreciate the offer, Taco, but I think I will sit this one out and let you guys take the lead. I am looking forward to a long-overdue and relaxing vacation, although I'm not sure how relaxing it will be after this news."

"I understand. I will be in the country, following the leads we get. We believe The Amir may be hiding somewhere in Western Europe under an assumed name, although we are still not sure what that name is yet. Take my number and call if you need anything or change your mind," Abbasi told him.

~~~

The would-be assassin arrived at work early. After the man dropped off the backpack last night, she made all the necessary plans for her part of the operation. She knew the office manager would not be in for another hour, and she found her way into his office, off the main check-in area of the hotel. She logged on to the hotel reservation software and found that the guest for Room 560, a Mr. John Spencer, had not checked in yet. The date had been changed to today. There were no notes in the reservation record regarding the change in check-in, and it wasn't her concern. She was here to do a job, and that job was about to be completed.

Emina took her backpack and master room card, used for housekeeping to gain access to the guest's room, and made her way up the elevator to the fifth floor. At this time of morning, most guests were still asleep, and the staff was minimal, so the chances of her being caught were slim.

She made her way down the hall to the last room in the right-hand corner of the building, No. 560.
~~~

She opened the door and walked in, ensuring that no one was in the room or had been. The record was correct: no one had checked into the room yet.

She took the combined device of Semtex and electronics out of her backpack and decided she would place the device along the inside edge of the door frame and set the sensors on the inside edge of the door. When the door was closed, the two sensors would touch and activate the device. When the door was next opened, it would disrupt the signal and set off the explosion.

She assumed the next person to walk through this door would be the man named John Spencer, today after three p.m.—which was the earliest he could check in. Once he opened the door, he would be checking out permanently.

Emina closed the door and made her way to the elevator. She wouldn't be showing up for work today.

Chapter 4

3:30 p.m.; Olga Stiller had worked in housekeeping at the Le Méridien for the past nine years. At fifty-five, it was hard to find a good job in Germany anymore. Age played a factor, regardless of whether employers wanted to hire you. She knew from her cousin, who lived in the United States, that such practices were against the law there, but not in Germany. Regardless, she was thankful to have the job. She had spent many years as a server and bartender at bars, disco-techs, and restaurants, mostly around the town of Fürth, a community just northwest of Nuremberg.

Fürth once housed the U.S. Army at Monteith Barracks, a helicopter airfield. Olga was younger and thinner back in those days and served American soldiers everywhere she worked. She even dated several of them back in the nineteen eighties. Germany was different back then.

There was no European Union; the Deutsche Mark was the currency instead of the euro. The economy wasn't thriving, but the American military spent a lot of money in the area—drinking, eating, renting apartments, etc. The only genuine problems Germans seemed to have at the time were all the Turkish immigrants.

To Olga, it seemed like remnants of the old Nazi regime. Everyone blamed some other ethnic group for their problems. Olga never really saw things that way. She always accepted that she was responsible for her own failures or successes in life, and truthfully, she was never that ambitious of a person. She never grew up with the drive or determination to be something more. Circumstances these days were a lot different.

These Middle Eastern immigrants Angela Merkel had allowed to flood into the country and Europe had caused concern for everyone. There had been women raped and abused, or beaten in the streets, one of whom she knew in the city. The Polizei didn't seem to actively handle those situations, at least not to the satisfaction of the German people. Elected officials stayed away from the subject; it was treated as "verboten."

Since World War II, the German people had been taught in school to be ashamed of their actions in the war and to accept that they were bad people. Speaking out against anyone of a different ethnic group, regardless of the circumstances and regardless of whether the issue had anything to do with their ethnicity, was unthinkable, and you would be considered a Nazi. Yes, things were very different these days. Olga found herself longing for a life a few decades in the past.

Olga's shift was almost finished. She had plans with her son after work. It was his birthday, and she had been working extra shifts to save for his birthday gift. Dieter had just graduated from university with his engineering degree. He was about to start work with one of Germany's largest engineering companies, which designed and built mechanical systems for manufacturing plants around the world.

Olga may not have had a lot of ambition in life, but her son did. He was the light of her life, and she was immensely proud of him. She had purchased a custom leather bag for him to carry his laptop and work in. It was something he had mentioned last year, but it was expensive, at least for her meager wages. However, she saved for months to buy it and let Dieter know how proud she was of him. They would celebrate tonight at home with his favorite schnitzel and heiße Kartoffelsalat, a type of German potato salad served warm and made with vinegar and bacon grease; it was Dieter's favorite. And, of course, her homemade streusel, which he had loved since he was a kid.

Olga approached the last room of the day to clean before clocking out. The fifth floor was her last floor, and room No. 560 was the last room on her list. She knew the room had been cleaned since the last guest; what a nasty individual he had been. The bedsheets had been soiled, undergarments had been left in the room, and they had not been clean garments, either.

Trash, empty bottles of beer and liquor, and day-old food containers were just lying around. It had made Olga sick to her stomach to clean that room. She had complained to her supervisor, but nothing had been done, and she doubted the guest had been charged for such an inconvenience to the hotel or its staff.

Olga wanted to make sure nothing had been missed during cleanup that the new guest might find when checking in today.

Olga lifted the master access card from the pulley string attached to her uniform and slid it into the key access slot on the door. The light turned green on the lock mechanism, and she turned the handle downward to open it. Then everything went dark.

~~~

Emina left her work and went back to her apartment in the St. Leonhard area of the city, just over a thirty-minute walk from the hotel. She was confident she had not been seen planting the explosives in room No. 560. And now, she had no need to return. She could start looking for her next assignment to assist the cause.

Arriving back at her apartment, she walked through the filth and trash that surrounded the complex.

This was indicative of such areas throughout Europe: entire sections of cities comprised mostly of immigrants who refused to assimilate into the countries in which they now lived, yet refused to give their allegiances.

Most of these people would never find a way to escape their misery. They would never learn the language or educate themselves to elevate their circumstances. Some, a small fraction, would; a very small fraction. The younger ones would be inspired by money, clothes, status, and other such frivolities and find a way to achieve it, either through hard work and persistence or through criminal activities such as drugs and trafficking.

She walked through the door of her building and up the three flights of old, worn stairs and flickering hall lights to her apartment. Upon opening the door to her one-room apartment, she found a note on the floor that had been slid under the door, with instructions to meet later in the day
~~~

at an abandoned factory south of town in the "Katzwanger Strasse" district.

Emina took a shower to wash off the sin of her actions and then made herself a breakfast of toast and hot tea. As she ate, she thought about the fact that she did not feel bad for those who would possibly lose their lives when the bomb went off. They were collateral damage, sometimes a necessity in achieving the objective. If they were believers, they would receive their rewards. If they were not believers, then they were exactly where they should be and received their justice accordingly.

After finishing her tea and getting dressed, Emina took the U-2 tram from the stop outside her apartment to the U-1 stop one block from the Mix Markt supermarket on Frankenstrasse and walked the remaining five blocks to the address she had been given.

The factory had been abandoned for what appeared to be a number of years. A chain-link fence lined the perimeter around the parking lot of the neglected facility.

As she walked along the sidewalk next to the fence, she found an opening at one edge of the fence about twenty yards from what used to be the main entrance to the business. She looked around to ensure there were no cars or witnesses to her going through the fence, which was technically breaking the law.

Once inside, she walked approximately seventy yards across a parking lot with weeds nearly the size of small trees that had grown up through the pavement. She realized she had assessed the area correctly. Indeed, no one had been here for quite some time, and there was little to no concern about anyone finding her here.

She walked along the outside of the old factory with broken windows and chained doors until she was on the backside, which faced the staging yard of a bus and truck manufacturing plant. There, she found a door that was not chained or locked and was slightly ajar. This was where she was supposed to enter.

Making her way inside, she found a dark, wide-open building with metal grates and staircases that were partially exposed. Old equipment from an assembly line of generations past was scattered throughout the open space. She walked around, looking for signs of the contact she was supposed to meet. There was just enough light coming in from the dirty and broken windows that she could make out her surroundings.

Finally, she noticed a faint yellow glow coming from the second floor. She found the metal staircase and made her way up the stairs. Once upstairs, she found the source of the glow. Coming from inside an old office, there was a small lamp on a desk, shining a dim hue across the room. She walked toward the office.

Emina walked through the door and found an old wooden desk and a metal chair with caster wheels that had been common during the nineteen-sixties and nineteen-seventies in such facilities. The lamp that was sitting on the desk was not really a lamp at all. It was more of a battery-operated portable light used for trekking or camping, as the Americans called it.

On the desk was an envelope. She took a few steps toward the desk, picked up the envelope, and opened it. Concentrating on pulling the piece of paper from the envelope, she never heard the footsteps of the man approaching her from behind.

He had been waiting in the shadows just outside the office, waiting for the woman to take the bait. He could not risk leaving loose ends, not now when he was so close, and no matter how loyal or useful that loose end might be.

Yes, he had to get rid of her. But it didn't mean he couldn't enjoy himself while doing so.

Emina opened the paper that had been inside and was confused by what she saw. It was blank. No letters, no writing. It took a moment for her brain to catch up with her eyes. By the time the thought occurred to her, she felt a sharp jolt of pain in her neck, and she faded into total darkness.

The man had used a handheld stun gun on the base of Emina's neck to disable her so he could take his time tying her up. Once the volts from the device hit the back of her neck and skull, she hit the floor, and the man could easily lift her and place her in the chair.

Using zip ties and rope, he strapped her to the chair. He didn't bother to use a gag. He was not worried if she woke up and screamed. The truth of the matter was he was looking forward to her screams. The pleasure he would get from her fear would feed his needs for at least a few days.

The power of having a life in your hands and bringing it to the edge of death and back again was a feeling like no other. Nothing compared to it. He took the most glee in seeing the hysterical realization in his victims' eyes.

Women provided so much more satisfaction as they didn't bargain for their lives the way men tended to. Men would offer things they could never actually provide: money, favors, sexual acts, all in exchange for a little more time in their wasted existence.

Women, on the other hand, instinctively understood the circumstances they were in, and the immediate fear of death shot to their eyes in a way that sent his pulse racing every time. The last act for him was when they realized death was not something that would come quickly, and they would reach a point where they begged him for it.

He looked at the utility pouch, now unrolled on the desk to his right. In each of the compartment sleeves were the instruments of his forthcoming endeavors. He had acquired them from, of all places, a global online shopping website: scalpels, blades, injection needles, tubes, a dental drill; forceps, and more. All with the click of a button. Abu-Sul Malik, as he was once referred to, could acquire almost anything he wanted to assist with his little vice.

Abu had once led a large majority within al-Qaeda. He had been revered and worked toward the political spectrum of the organization, trying to gain importance and status in a group widely known throughout the world as "terrorists."

He made the decision years ago, after he learned of Operation Grasshopper, in which three Americans and two Afghans had found him in Tora Bora, to change his appearance and use a lookalike to keep himself alive. Luckily for him, it worked.

A couple of years later, when the so-called "elite" Navy SEALs, Team Six, had reportedly killed the Amir, he was safely starting his new life while his loyal doppelgänger was being filled with the infidels' bullets. They never even bothered to check DNA to make sure it was him. He was indeed fortunate and rewarded for his faithful path.

Once his body double was securely in place, a martyr to the cause who had been a loyal follower for several years and had no family to be concerned about, Abu-Sul Malik made his way across the border of

Pakistan using the new passport and IDs he had paid for through the Afghan government officials he had bribed.

He traveled south to Hyderabad, where he spent a couple of months in a small section of the city, monitoring details of his "death" and awaiting any further information on identifying his supposed body.

It seemed the Americans and Westerners in Europe were too busy celebrating his demise to verify the body was indeed his.

Once he felt certain they were not continuing to search for him, he made his way along the coast on N10 until he arrived at Tamp Kuh on the Pakistan-Iran border.

He reached out to one Iranian official he had dealt with many times as a "financier" of sorts. Iran helped fund many of the "activities" the Amir had been involved with over the years. They were less concerned about who and how things were done; they were more concerned with loyalty as a proxy for Iranian leadership and with seeing results of destruction toward the West and Israel.

The Amir's contact in Iran ensured his safe passage across the border and helped secure housing for him in Bandar-Abbas, a city on the coast of Southern Iran, directly across the straits from Oman.

After a few months of what felt like house arrest to the Amir, he began plotting his revenge, his Jihad against those who had tried to kill him. "Praise be to Allah" for sparing his life and allowing him to continue his calling of killing the infidels and non-believers.

He started making boat trips from Bandar-Abbas to Kumzar, Oman. Abu-Sul Malik would then make his way through Dubai to the rest of Oman and on toward Yemen, where he had many contacts who had been loyal servants in the past for training soldiers of Allah and martyrs alike for him.

He was not ready to reveal his true identity but used details and information from previous relationships and contacts to lend himself credence with those aligned with him.

He knew it would be imprudent to reveal himself too quickly and to too many or to the wrong people. He would choose only a few extremely loyalists to know his true identity and whom he would allow to run and control his new organization.

Now? Now he was on that path—one in which he did not serve the ambitions of leadership and fame. Now he served himself and his desire for more personal pleasures, like what he was about to do to the beautiful woman strapped to the chair in front of him. Once he completed his mission of revenge, finding the last remaining members of Operations Grasshopper, nothing else would distract him.

His anticipation was getting the better of him. Time to wake her up.

Chapter 5

3:31 PM. As Spencer and Abbasi exited the restaurant, they stood there momentarily, looking at one another in front of the entrance. Abbasi extended his hand toward Spencer to say goodbye when they heard what sounded like a large blast. The sound was muffled, indicating it was not very close, but as these two men were all too aware, it was the sound of an explosion.

At that moment, Abbasi's cell phone rang.

"Yes," Abbasi said as he answered. His eyes widened as they shifted toward Spencer.

Spencer could see by the look on his former teammate's face that this had something to do with what they had just been talking about.

Abbasi put the phone back in his pocket.

"No more wondering. It was the Le Méridien. The explosion was on the same floor as the room under your name. I'm betting the explosion detonated from your room."

Spencer stood there, somewhat in disbelief, feeling like Al Pacino in a mafia movie. He had been out for ten years, and the happier for it. Now he was being pulled back in against his will.

"Shit!"

"Come on, we'll take a taxi; it'll be quicker," Abbasi said while walking toward the main street without bothering to see if Spencer was following.

Spencer started following the man he trusted without giving it a moment's thought. The two hailed a taxi, and Abbasi gave the driver their intended destination. "Le Méridien, Mach Schnell," which was a way of letting the driver know in German that they were in a hurry.

~~~

3:58 PM. The fire crew had determined the staircase of the hotel to be structurally safe as a means for people making their way out of the hotel and for emergency personnel making their way in to investigate. The elevator had been shut down for safety purposes, which was protocol around most of the world in such events.

Agent Hall made his way up to the fifth floor to room number 560. He walked into the room to make a firsthand account of what was left and what he observed. The room was only partially intact. The windows and window frames on the far wall had been blown out, leaving a gaping hole that had once framed a picturesque view of the Nuremberg Hauptbahnhof Train Station. A queen-sized bed that had been at the door's edge was ripped to pieces, and the wooden dresser and chairs that had been in the room were blown apart.

The agent walked around the room slowly and methodically, making sure not to disturb any potential evidence or cause any additional damage.

Agent Hall coordinated with the Incident Commander for the Berufsfeuerwehr, which translated to "Professional Fire Brigade." This particular level of fire service was used in larger cities.

The commander determined that the blast had originated at the door to the room. It appeared to have been rigged to go off when the door was opened.

Apparently, we are on the right track, thought Agent Hall as he made his way out of the room and back down the staircase and out the door of the hotel to wait for his boss.

~~~

4:23 PM. The taxi dropped Spencer and Abbasi off at the main intersection of Marienstasse and Konigstorgraben, two blocks from the hotel. Traffic all over the city was backing up due to concerns about potentially more explosions. The taxi had to let the two men off here, as there was no way to make it to the hotel.

Emergency vehicles were still arriving, and the Polizei were starting to block traffic and pedestrians from making their way toward the hotel.

The scene was pure chaos but organized, especially with the Germans managing the situation. A couple of international news vans had pulled across the street from where Spencer and Abbasi were exiting the taxi.

Ambulances, fire trucks, police, hotel staff, and guests crowded around the outer perimeter, at least those who hadn't been killed or were being transported to the hospital.

Abbasi motioned for Spencer to follow him to the corner across the street from the hotel, in front of a local fitness studio on the back side of the hotel.

Abbasi walked up to a slender but athletic man with dark blonde hair, who appeared to be in his thirties. The man was wearing what could be described as business casual attire for Europe: dark jeans and comfortable dress-style shoes, a light blue shirt, and a casual dark blue sport coat.

"Spencer, this is Charley Hall. Charley is one of us. He's assigned to the RSO's office as a 'Legal Attaché.' I recruited him from Stanford before he finished law school," said Abbasi, making the introduction.

"A hell of a lot more exciting than filing briefs for a living," said Charley as he extended his hand to Spencer. "Sorry, you're supposed to be on the receiving end of this fireworks display."

"Have we verified?" asked Abbasi.

"Yes, looks like the detonation was from Room No. 560, activated when someone opened the door. We assume at this point it was housekeeping going into the room that set it off," Agent Hall replied.

"Damn it. How many lost so far?" asked Spencer.

"It's not clear at this time, but accounting for occupancy records, staff scheduled to be on the floor, and those guests not accounted for yet, we think somewhere around 15-20 people. We will know more in the next hour or two."

"How did you know so fast to call Abbasi?" Spencer wanted to know.

Charley glanced toward Abbasi, who gave a slight nod.

"We have had a team watching the hotel the day before you landed to look for any signs of the Amir or his group. We needed to be sure, and apparently, some at the agency wanted to make certain you were safe."

"You've been staking out my hotel for two days?" Spencer said, more of a statement than a question, looking at Abbasi.

"Technically, it's three if you account for the time difference," replied Abbasi, trying to soften the situation with a bit of sarcasm.

"What do we know, and what's the plan?" Spencer directed back at Abbasi.

"That's a conversation for somewhere else," he replied.

Abbasi's cell phone rang. He quickly answered and responded.

"Understood. Bring an extra overnight bag." He hit the end button on the phone and placed it back inside his coat pocket.

Abbasi looked at Spencer with an unasked question on his face.

Spencer nodded in the affirmative and said, "Too late now, I'm in, whether I like it or not. All the way."

Abbasi told Charley to have a driver meet them back at the intersection where the taxi had dropped them off, to which Charley made a quick call that Spencer couldn't hear and didn't try to.

Charley nodded to Abbasi and hung up the call.

Abbasi responded to Charley with a nod of his head toward the hotel.

"Stay on it."

Charley nodded back and looked to Spencer. "Stay safe," then jogged across the street toward the hotel.

"Let's go," said Abbasi, and the two walked back toward Marienstrasse to catch their ride. To where, Spencer wasn't sure, but he assumed an agency safe house somewhere in the city or close by.

A fairly normal practice for the CIA was to have a number of "safe" houses in and around a major city of operation, strategically located for different reasons.

They were either located close to areas of normal operations or in places where most people, even those looking for you, didn't want to go.

Spencer and Abbasi climbed into the back seat of the black Mercedes Benz, and the driver started making his way through the city center traffic toward the B14 highway. It took them forty minutes to get out of the city due to the traffic and emergency vehicles still heading toward the hotel. Once out of the center of town, they drove toward the B14 highway and continued southwest.

They eventually turned north just past a gas station in the town of Petersaurach and zigzagged through small farming communities and country roads for approximately an hour and a half, which Spencer knew was backtracking to ensure they were not being followed.

Finally arriving at a corner house in a small community in the town of Weihenzell, the house was two stories with a large parking area and a small barn. The property also had an 'L' shaped, constructed stall-style storage area. It was a modern version of a traditional German home and sat at a three-way intersection, which provided them multiple egress routes but could also trap them from three different directions if attacked.

The driver pulled into the large driveway, parking the car where three other vehicles were parked: a late-model dark blue Volkswagen Jetta, a slightly worn-looking white Euro work van that seemed about fifteen years old, and a black Audi A6 crossover.

The sun had set, and it was now dusk. A slight drizzle was starting to fall. Abbasi motioned for Spencer to get out of the car, and both men exited the vehicle.

"I hope this isn't awkward for you," Abbasi said.

"What, having a terrorist hold a personal vendetta against me for something we never followed up on in the first place?"

"No," said Abbasi, "Me running this operation."

Spencer looked at him, somewhat confused. "Why would that be awkward for me?"

"Well, the last time we worked together, I was on loan to the agency and reported to you as the Field Officer of the operation."

"Clearly, you don't know enough about me to realize I don't give a shit about such things. You proved yourself in my eyes during Operation Grasshopper, enough for me to trust you. You're a brother in arms and a damn fine soldier from what I saw back then. From what I see now, you take the job seriously and lead your team well. Since we are talking about my life in this situation, I'll give you my opinion when I feel it's needed. Otherwise … your monkeys, your circus."

Abbasi gave a slight smile and a nod of thanks in Spencer's direction and motioned toward the front steps of the house.

Abbasi knocked on the door. Spencer found it a bit odd that the Senior Field Officer would knock at his own safe house.

A pleasant-looking woman in her mid-to-late sixties, with short gray hair and glasses, answered the door and warmly greeted them as they stepped inside.

"John," the woman said with surprise and a German accent in her voice, as she reached out and hugged him like a long-lost family member or friend. There was something oddly gratifying about it to him.

"Wie geht es dir?" Abbasi asked the woman.

"Wunderbar," she replied. "Come in, come in."

Once the door was closed, the woman turned toward Abbasi, who had taken off his coat and handed it to her. She looked at Spencer for a long moment, then slightly grinned and nodded her head toward the hallway, walking off with Abbasi's coat.

"Well, that was interesting," said Spencer. "Friend of yours?"

"It's about to become more interesting," replied Abbasi, "and a friend of yours as well."

Spencer assumed Abbasi meant that she was a member of the team and would be a benefit to them. Still, there was something familiar about the woman he couldn't put his finger on, but he had more important issues to think about at the moment—namely his life.

The two men heard voices coming from down the hallway and walked through the somewhat narrow corridor into a large, open kitchen with a traditional German table and wall-mounted benches, where a group of five men sat talking in both German and English.

Once Spencer and Abbasi walked in, two of the men sitting in chairs stood and walked out, leaving two seats for Spencer and Abbasi.

The woman walked into the kitchen, and the man sitting at the head of the table on the bench directly across from Spencer looked at him but spoke to the woman. "Bring Spencer a Cola-Weissen."

Spencer knew that Cola-Weissen was the general term used in this part of Germany for a mixture of half Hefeweizen beer and Cola. He knew this because it used to be his favorite drink back when he was stationed in Germany with 10th Group in the nineteen-eighties; it allowed

Spencer to enjoy a few beers without getting hammered in case they got called back to base. He even continued to drink it when he rotated back to 3rd Group in the U.S. … then it hit him.

"Holy shit!"

Chapter 6

"Well, it took you long enough, Spencer," said the man sitting at the table.

"Danny?" Spencer said, almost as a question, as he slowly stood up to embrace the man now standing at the other end of the table.

"Jesus, you've aged, and your hair grew long."

"Yeah, and you've gotten fat and forgetful," was Danny's retort.

Both men burst out laughing and embraced one another again, like only men with their history could.

"How long has it been? Ten or twelve years?" Spencer asked.

"Closer to seventeen, Spencer," said Danny.

"I can't believe it's been that long. It's not possible," Spencer said, looking down and to the side as if searching for an explanation of the timeline and feeling guilty for losing touch with the man who had been like a big brother and father figure to him.

"I… I'm uh… I'm sorry, Danny," Spencer stammered, heartfelt remorse in his words for losing touch.

The woman set the Cola-Weissen on the table in front of Spencer, and he finally realized who she was and felt equally ashamed about Danny.

"Gretta. I can't believe I didn't recognize you. I'm such an ass. Please forgive me."

"Well, I was a little younger and hotter seventeen years ago, John. Plus, I was a few pounds lighter and had more hair," she laughed and gave Spencer a welcoming kiss on the cheek, as old, meaningful friends do. “The years change us all.”

“The haircut definitely threw me off more than anything else,” he responded.

“Cancer will do that to you,” she replied somewhat light-heartedly, walking back to the kitchen sink.

Spencer stood there in shock watching her as she walked away, overwhelmed by having just been reunited with two of the closest people in his life once upon a time. And then hearing one of them had cancer that he didn’t know about and hadn’t been there for … his guilt stabbed him in the gut like a knife.

He looked up at Danny, visibly distraught by what he had just heard.

“Breast cancer. She had a double mastectomy seven years ago. She’s better now, John. She has been in remission for a few years.”

“I’m such an asshole, Danny. I should have been there for you guys,” Spencer said.

“You couldn’t have known, Spencer. Life gets in the way of us all and takes us in different directions we never expected or can explain,” Danny said.

Spencer’s mind wandered with thoughts about how he lost touch with Danny and Gretta and why he never reached out during all the years that had passed.

After Spencer’s divorce, someone in his life had let him down and hurt him again; he began to implode. He started drinking too much and convinced himself that everyone else would eventually leave him, like his mother and wife had done. He even convinced himself that Danny and Gretta would eventually turn on him as well, so he chose to eliminate the threat before it had a chance to happen.

It had been a painful downward spiral. He found unhealthy ways to cope with his circumstances. Everything happened around the time he was leaving the Army. Spencer packed up what he had left and moved away right after his military separation was finalized. He walked away from his career and from everyone in his life at the time.

The warrior in him finally came to its senses, and Spencer eventually got his act together. He began working with the Agency and felt so guilty and embarrassed about his behavior toward Danny and Gretta that he never reached out to them. That decision was causing more regret now, at this moment, than he could ever have imagined. But for now, he had to push those feelings aside as best he could.

"I don't understand. What are you guys doing here at the safe house in Germany?" Spencer asked, genuinely confused.

"Well, number one, it's not a safe house, per se. I mean, it is a safe house. But it's not an Agency safe house," Danny replied, toying with Spencer now.

"That makes no sense. What do you mean it's a safe house but not an Agency safe house?"

Danny replied, "It is our home, Spencer. Gretta and I live here. We have for fifteen years."

"Your home? You guys were in Fayetteville the last time I saw you. You were talking about staying somewhere in the community and doing some contract training and armory work with the teams when you retired."

"And why the hell are we all in your home as an Ops Center/Safe House with a scumbag tracking me down to kill me? This is putting you guys in harm's way." Spencer said, a little worked up because of his concern for his long-lost friends.

"Friends" wasn't exactly an accurate description of the relationship he had with Danny and Gretta. Danny was almost thirteen years older than Spencer and had been assigned as his mentor when Spencer did his first rotation from 10th Group in Germany to 3rd Group at Fort Bragg, North Carolina.

Even though Spencer had learned to trust his team and value being part of a brotherhood, he was still very closed off to any personal connections back in those days. After the childhood he had, he doubted he would ever really trust anyone in that way.

Danny saw something in Spencer he had seen in a few other guys over the years—guys who had difficult upbringings, like Spencer. Closed off to the world but hell-bent on proving themselves and their strength. Some of the men had chips on their shoulders aimed at everyone and everything around them but could leave it at the door when it came to training and operating; otherwise, they wouldn't have made the selection.

But Spencer was a little different in Danny's eyes and reminded him of his older brother who had died in Vietnam.

Danny took Spencer under his wing, and over the course of the rotation, Danny became more like a big brother and almost a father figure to Spencer. Gretta, Danny's wife, who was originally from Germany, couldn't have children and took on a bit of a motherly role in Spencer's life.

They were the closest thing to "family" he had ever known, and he felt guilt and pain at not having recognized them tonight or kept in touch throughout all these years, let alone the apology he owed them for just leaving without so much as a goodbye. He would need to have that conversation with them later once this situation with the Amir was resolved, assuming he lived through it.

"I reached out to Danny when we realized you were possibly a target of Abu Sul-Malik," Abbasi offered.

"How would you have even known to contact Danny about me, and why?" asked Spencer.

"Because we met at the 'Farm' when I did some training for the Agency with new recruits," Danny said.

"Since we were both former ODA, we connected and shared a few meals and drinks. I'd mentioned I had done a previous operation when on active duty, and during the conversation, your name came up," Abbasi replied.

"What are the odds?" Danny said with a short laugh under his breath.

"And you decide to bring them into a potentially life-threatening situation to help save my ass?" Spencer directed at Abbasi with slight anger.

"It was our choice, Spencer," replied Danny, cutting off a potential argument.

"Both of ours," Gretta spoke up, having walked into the conversation without Spencer noticing.

Spencer glanced at Gretta, who looked at him with nothing but compassion and a bit of moisture in her eyes. The kind of look he supposed one gives toward a beloved family member in need or in pain.

And a look he surely did not deserve and did not want because of the pain and guilt it was causing him.

Danny looked at Abbasi and made a slight nod toward the hall.

"Let's check the perimeter and give me a brief," said Abbasi to the remaining two men at the table. With that, the two men stood, and the three of them left the room.

Now it was just Spencer, Danny, and Gretta standing in the kitchen together, looking at each other in silence.

~~~

Danny Doyle was 69 years old.

He grew up in Cincinnati, Ohio, the youngest of two boys to John and Caroline Doyle. Danny's father had been a high school history teacher and deacon of their church, and his mother had been an English teacher at the junior high school just down the street from their house.

He and his brother Donnie, who was seven years older than Danny, had very normal Midwestern lives growing up. They went to school, played baseball, went to church, rode their bicycles through the neighborhoods, and went swimming. Their parents raised them with strong values of right and wrong and instilled in them the importance of supporting others and their community.

Donnie joined the Army at eighteen, volunteering to go to Vietnam instead of waiting on the draft. Danny remembered being very proud of his big brother. He had looked up to Donnie all of his life. His brother had been a thrill-seeker growing up, whether jumping a ramp on his bicycle, jumping off a cliff into the water, or always willing to jump in the middle of a fight to protect the small guy being picked on.

Donnie died in a night ambush during his fourth month in Vietnam. Danny missed his brother.

Danny, like his brother, joined the Army and became a career soldier who spent more than twenty years on active duty, eighteen of which were in the Special Forces.

He started his team career as an 18-Bravo, or what was referred to as a Weapons Sergeant in the teams. He trained and specialized in domestic and international small arms and light and heavy crew-served weapons, as well as anti-aircraft and anti-armor weapons. As the weapons sergeant, he
~~~

also employed an array of conventional and unconventional warfare tactics.

Danny eventually made his way up the ranks, being promoted to 18-Zulu, Special Forces Senior Sergeant, supervising and instructing enlisted member activities and serving as the liaison in joint and coalition missions, responsible for planning and operations for higher headquarters and joint commands. He enjoyed the challenge and the confidence that had been placed in him, but more so, the honor of looking out for the men he was responsible for.

John Spencer had come to 3rd Group about halfway through Sergeant Doyle's career, and he had been assigned to show him the ropes and mentor him.

Even though Spencer had just finished his first rotation at 10th Group in Germany, 3rd Group had a different level of responsibilities and a different theater of operation which provided for an alternate way of operating and differing standards of performance.

Spencer would need to learn to "gel" within the confines of a new group of twelve operators, and Danny was assigned to help ensure the transition was a smooth one.

Since Spencer was coming from Germany, Danny thought a home-cooked meal by his wonderful German wife, Gretta, would be a nice way to get Spencer off to a good start.

Spencer turned out to be a quick study and eager to make a positive impact on the team. The more time the two spent together, the more Danny began to take Spencer under his wing. Danny developed an interesting connection with Spencer—one that was a combination of parent and big brother.

The two developed a strong bond, as did Gretta. She used to fuss over Spencer like he was her own child. Although Danny and Gretta were only about thirteen years older than Spencer, he was like the son they never had or could ever have. It was an unusual relationship, but a strong one. They were a family.

When Spencer and Cindy got engaged, Gretta had a lot of reservations. She always thought Spencer was just playing the field and having fun, as a lot of the guys on the team did. But when Spencer proposed, Gretta told Danny it was a mistake. Cindy was not the type of woman to handle the hardships of being a team wife. She promised Danny at the time that she would never bring it up to Spencer because she didn't want to sound disapproving and hurt him.

Spencer had opened up to Gretta and Danny about his childhood one night at their house, sharing how abusive his father had been and how he never heard from his mother after she left. The last thing Gretta wanted to do was disappoint him by being discouraging about his relationship with Cindy.

Spencer rotated between 10th Group and 3rd Group a couple of times over the years. All the while, the three of them remained as close as family until Cindy filed for divorce. Spencer was on rotation with 3rd Group when Cindy told him she was looking for something more in life than he could provide on a soldier's salary, and she did not want to spend the rest of her life moving back and forth between bases.

It hit Spencer hard and seemed to come out of left field; he had not expected it and thought everything was okay between them. One day while Spencer was training at the team's clearing house, Cindy showed up and cleared out the house. She took everything except for Spencer's clothes and an old lounge chair. She had packed up everything in a U-Haul and moved to Florida.

Spencer went into a bit of a downward spiral after that. In the coming days and weeks, he withdrew from Danny and Gretta. Danny convinced Gretta that his teammate and friend needed space to deal with his issues on his own. Danny helped cover for Spencer a few times when he showed up at the unit still drunk or didn't show up at all.

Within a matter of days after the divorce was final, Spencer had turned in his paperwork for early retirement and was gone. He never said a word to Danny or Gretta. That was almost seventeen years ago, and Danny felt like Spencer was the Prodigal Son returning home.

~~~

"Please forgive me. I have no excuses other than my foolishness and pride," said Spencer. These kinds of conversations and emotions were not supposed to be had by men like him and Danny—men who had trained, fought, and been the tip of the spear for so many years. They were warriors, not emotional guys with man-buns and pronouns.
~~~

But that was another life—one he had not been a part of for many years now. His instincts and training were the same: still sharp, still aware, and still capable, even if a few pounds heavier. But he was tired—tired of living a life void of trust and family.

And that's exactly what Danny and Gretta were to him: "family"—one he walked away from due to no fault of their own. They never let him down. They never hurt him. But after Cindy left him, he told himself it was only a matter of time before it happened, and he made the decision one night, along with a bottle of scotch, to cut all ties.

Spencer felt something wet on his cheek and moved his hand to swipe it away. Emotion had finally broken through the tough exterior of this old warrior. He suddenly felt Gretta's arms wrapped around him in a warm embrace filled with love and forgiveness. He couldn't hold it in any longer and, although quietly, allowed himself to sob, if only for the moment.

"We love you, John. Always did. There is nothing to forgive you for," Gretta told him with all the warmth of a mother to a child.

"We're family, Spencer, or as close as we are allowed to be. We are here for you and always have been. Seventeen years isn't going to change that," Danny reassured his old friend.

This is what 'real' family is, Spencer thought to himself. They could have yelled at him. They could have shrugged when Abbasi told them he was in trouble; Danny and Gretta could have done any number of things differently from what they were doing now. Nothing else in his life had given him the feeling of family more than at that moment, and he felt blessed for it.

"Now sit down and drink your Cola-Weissen and tell us what you have been up to," said Gretta, pointing to the beer and the chair.

The three friends sat there catching up on everything from John's career changes and his bachelor existence to Gretta's cancer and her and Danny moving back to Germany.

They talked and laughed into the late hours of the night.

Abbasi left them to catch up and didn't intrude for the remainder of the night. His men pulled shifts, walking the perimeter of the property and staying in the shed area that served as a makeshift command center.

Chapter 7

Spencer woke the next morning feeling better and lighter than he had felt for most of his life. Although somewhat embarrassed by his show of emotions, it seemed to heal and cleanse him. It was as if a barricade had been lifted from his life, giving him the ability to move forward or start over—maybe even truly start for the first time.

He made his way down the hall to the bathroom and took a quick shower. Back in his room, he changed clothes. He hadn't thought about it last night until he walked into his room to go to bed. His suitcase, laptop, and backpack from Frau Knopf's Gasthaus were sitting on his bed. Apparently, Abbasi had his men pick up Spencer's things after the blast at the Le Meridien and transport them here before he had arrived.

Spencer had to hand it to Abbasi; so far, he had thought of everything and truly seemed on top of his game. Abbasi was closer to Danny's age than to Spencer's, and Spencer was thinking this might well be Abbasi's last operation before retirement.

Typically, men of his age didn't continue in field work, and if you were in field work at that age, it was a sure thing you weren't in consideration for an executive role or a political appointment. Regardless, Abbasi had earned Spencer's approval and, as difficult as it was, his trust.

Spencer's stomach growled as he hadn't eaten dinner last night and hadn't eaten anything since lunch yesterday with Abbasi. Damn, that pork shoulder was good, he thought. You just couldn't get things like that back home. BBQ pork, sure, but a roasted pork shoulder or pork shank like you get in Europe… He could smell food coming from the kitchen downstairs and assumed it would include coffee.

He made his way downstairs and into the kitchen, where he found Gretta, Danny, and Abbasi sitting at the table eating. Serving dishes with eggs, bacon, toast, cheese, marmalade, and sliced tomatoes were spread across the table, along with a pot of coffee.

"I see life in the corporate world got you used to sleeping late," Danny said with a smile.

"I'm retired; no need to set an alarm anymore," Spencer replied.

"I've been retired for years and still get up around six a.m.," stated Danny.

"That's old age and prostate," quipped Gretta. At that, they all chuckled out loud.

Gretta started fixing Spencer a plate and handed it to him. Spencer thanked her and poured himself a cup of coffee.

"So, what's the game plan?" asked Spencer, directing his question at Abbasi.

"I'm awaiting word from my team in Nuremberg regarding who they believe placed the bomb in your room. We believe there is an active group in the city—possibly a sleeper cell that's been activated. There has been little chatter to this point, so we are behind the eight ball on this one. The total death toll is at eight."

"Any leads?" Spencer wanted to know.

"None yet. At least none that we can connect to the Amir or his group directly."

"Have you checked to see if any of the staff failed to show up to work yesterday, those who were scheduled to be there when the bomb went off?" asked Spencer.

"That's what we are waiting on now. Luckily, the blast was contained within that section of the fifth floor. The bottom floors and lobby areas are all fine, so it shouldn't be hard to get those details. The engineers and safety personnel have cleared the rest of the building for use, from the first to the third floor. They have evacuated the fourth floor as a precaution, and the hotel has moved those guests and any others who wanted to switch hotels wherever they could. But with the climate conference getting ready to start, there are hardly any available rooms in the city," Abbasi informed him.

"How sure are we that this attack was directed at Spencer versus someone else on that floor or in the hotel who is here for the conference?" asked Danny.

"Fairly certain," was Abbasi's response. "At present, only a few government officials had checked into the hotel at the time of the blast, and none of them are of a level that would warrant a direct hit."

"Could it have been a statement by a climate terrorist group?" Danny questioned.

"No evidence at this time, and they would have waited until the conference started to make such a statement. In fact, no groups are claiming responsibility or even beating their chests online, which is odd. Some of these groups try to lay claim to anything they can, whether they had anything to do with it or not, just to gain mention in the news and try to build credibility," Abbasi informed him. But he was pretty sure Danny already knew this.

"Well, until someone opens fire or blows up the barn, I'm going to enjoy my breakfast," was Spencer's contribution. "Right now, eggs and bacon are worth more than 77 virgins in the afterlife."

Abbasi's phone rang. He answered it immediately and stood up to walk away from the table.

~~~

Abu-Sul-Malik sat at a small Middle Eastern café in the heart of Pristina, Kosovo, drinking an Arabica coffee.

His plan was to use the remaining look-alike double he had used before the elite infidel group of Navy SEALs took out his compound in Pakistan and his most loyal followers. But he soon learned he had other followers whom he could trust—men who were more faithful than he could have imagined. They protected him during his surgery to mask his true identity and ensured his wishes were carried out exactly as if he were the prophet himself.

It was one of those men he was sitting in this café to meet with. Someone who was not on a watch list or a suspect of any international organization. In fact, this man was a European citizen and had been working on the American base for the past several years in Human
~~~

Resources. He had access to all the personnel records on the base in Kosovo.

The Amir had met his mother while in Kosovo twenty-five years ago. Abu had made his way into the country under the guise of a Saudi group helping to build mosques and schools for the Albanian Muslims in the country after the war. What he was really doing was looking for recruits and places to train those recruits and house members of his group in an effort to attack Europe.

Selma was a server at a small café who had caught his attention. Although Muslim, he was not prone to denying himself pleasures of the flesh, in multiple respects, apparently. He developed a relationship of convenience with Selma while he was there. Unlike his other interests in women, this one was purely sexual, and she became pregnant.

He had thought to kill her and get rid of the problem altogether but decided it might be beneficial to have an offspring born in Europe. That could prove useful, as long as no one knew about him being the father. Abu made an agreement with Selma; he would pay her to raise the child. He would give her enough money to have a decent life and provide an education for the child, as long as she told no one who he was.

The Amir thought that if the child was male, he could eventually make himself known as the father and raise the boy under his own ideals so he could be of use in the future. If the child were a girl, he might have her and her mother both killed. Women were less dependable and emotional, in his opinion, and were harder to trust. This, however, was a risk he felt was worth taking and one he could resolve quickly if needed.

Goran, Abu Sul-Malik's son, was twenty-four years old, five feet ten inches tall, slender, and athletic with bushy dark hair. The boy played soccer throughout his youth as his favorite pastime with his friends.

He learned English and German during his early academic years and went to university in Tuzla, where he studied human resource management and minored in business.

Goran's mother had never married and raised him as a single mother. He had a much better life than most of his friends. Their apartment was bigger, nicer, and well-furnished. His mother had a car—nothing fancy—but most of the women in their town, especially single women and mothers, could not afford such a luxury. And they always had enough food to eat. Goran's mother never spoke of his father, and the boy assumed he had been killed in the war, like many of his friends' fathers had been.

When he was eight years old, Goran was taken out of class at the community madrasa where he went to school and was brought into a room with a man who was seated in a chair. The man introduced himself as Goran's father and told him that he could call him 'Babai,' which was Albanian for 'father.' This way, if anyone ever questioned him, or if he ever spoke about his father, no one would make the connection with Abu Sul-Malik.

He had told Goran that he wasn't able to see him very often because he was a very important man, and many people were trying to hurt him. The man said he stayed away because he didn't want anyone to hurt Goran or his mother. So, he told his son he had to stay away to keep them safe, but he would try to see him as much as he could.

His father told him he had men who would keep watch over them to keep them safe, and sometimes he would send messages to Goran through these men. He would use a code word that only Goran and he would know. That way, he would know it was from his father. The code word was 'Shahid.'

He gave the boy a small present of Turkish delights and told him not to mention their visit to his mother or anyone else. Their safety depended on it.

Goran was only eight years old, but he understood the meaning of being safe, growing up in a community that was still recovering from war, where many of his mother's family and his friends' family and parents had been killed. He knew the meaning of such things too early in his life.

The boy was happy to know he had a father who was alive and that he was an important man. Goran told himself he would help keep his father safe and would not tell anyone about their visit. When Abu Sul-Malik stood up, the child jumped up and hugged him before his father walked away. The embrace meant everything to the young Goran but meant nothing at all to the man on the receiving end.

His father sent him many messages over the years, even providing him with private schooling to ensure he had a proper Muslim education and knew his history regarding infidels. His father made several trips over the years to visit with him. Each time it was a brief visit, but one of meaning to his son, as he knew his father was risking his life to visit.

As Goran grew older and matured in his age and education, his father began treating him more as a man and less as a child. He showed the boy love but was not an affectionate man. His trust and respect were more the forms of love his father showed, and the more trust he showed Goran, the more he felt loved by his father.

When Goran was about to turn sixteen, he received word through one of his father's men that his Babai would not look the same the next time they saw one another. He would appear to be someone different, but he should trust that he would make himself known to his son, and for Goran to trust him. This was for both of their safety.

The fact that his father was asking him for his trust and sharing this secret was not lost on Goran. He felt as if his father was giving him the ultimate gift of his trust and, thereby, his love. The young man would do anything for his father at this point. His father had always made it clear to him that he must succeed in his education and that he must go to university.

His father always told Goran that what he learned about infidels and the Quran, he must not show in his daily life. He had to be friendly to the outside world so they would never know who he was or his knowledge of what they, the infidels, had done to his people. There would be a time and place for such things.

Goran was in university and eighteen before he ever saw his father again.

He was sitting in a café in Tuzla, having a coffee and studying for an exam, when a gentleman stopped at his table and asked what he was reading.

“I am studying for an exam,” the young man replied.

“What courses are you studying?” asked the man.

Goran felt something familiar about the man but could not quite understand why.

“Human Resources,” the student replied.

“Are you a good student?” the man asked.

“Yes, I try to be,” was his response. His father had always told him to study hard and learn, but not to stand out.

"Try to stay just above the middle of your classes so you don't draw too much attention to yourself," was his father's advice.

"You're not excelling too much, are you, my son?" questioned the man.

Goran jerked his head up from his book and stared at the man. He did not recognize him. His facial lines were different: a slender, clean-shaven face, smaller nose, all gray hair nicely cut and styled, and wearing a gray suit. But he instinctively knew who this gentleman was.

"Babai?" he asked in anticipation.

"Shahid" was his father's reply, said with a smile.

Goran had never known his father's real name, as he had never been told, and he had never asked. Therefore, he had never learned who his father really was until he was sixteen.

The story of the American special forces killing the terrorist mastermind, Abu Sul-Malik, was worldwide news. From the largest cities to the smallest villages, the news had been everywhere. That was the first time he truly understood who his father was.

There, on the television news at home, was his father's image. Dressed in traditional clothing, the man he knew as "Babai" was revealed to be a terrorist known throughout the world. The next image he saw on television that night was a picture of his father's dead body. Then, an image of both pictures side by side. Goran was distraught, believing his father was dead. The man he had come to know and love was now gone, killed by the infidels.

The following morning, one of his father's men stopped him on his way to school to assure him that his father was alive and to remind him not to say anything to anyone. No one must know. His father sent messages through these men, telling him it was too dangerous to call him. But, in time, he would be in touch and to trust him.

~~~

Goran would do anything for his father.

Even now, as he walked toward the café in Nuremberg, where he was to meet his father. He knew the bombing at the hotel was partly due to his delivering the backpack and explosives to the woman at her apartment. He did not know her but assumed she was one of his father's
~~~

faithful. He was here to help his father conduct Allah's justice on the non-believers and the infidels who tried to kill his "Babai."

Chapter 8

Abbasi's team had verified that the blast did indeed come from the room reserved under John Spencer's name. It was a sensor-triggered device activated by the hotel housekeeping assistant trying to prepare the room for Spencer's check-in.

"Two members of the staff had not shown up for work today," said Abbasi. "Both are supposedly from Kosovo. One is a woman, about forty years old, who worked as a housekeeping supervisor named 'Lena Markovich' from Pristina.

We identified her from hotel video footage. Her real name is Emina Begić, who is actually a Bosnian from Sarajevo. The Serbs killed her parents during Milosevic's genocide. She is on a watchlist of suspected terrorists who have been targeting known Serbian militants involved in the attack on Bosnia."

"I guess it's safe to say she's not a suspected terrorist anymore," Spencer chimed in. "But what does a Serbian terrorist have to do with the Amir?"

"We don't know the answer to that yet," Abbasi replied. Looking back down at his pocket-sized notepad where he had written the information, he continued. "The other is a younger male named Avni Shala, in his early twenties, who worked at the front desk. He is from Pristina, Kosovo, but we cannot find a connection suggesting they knew each other."

"Maybe not, but it's a bit of a coincidence that they are both from Kosovo and both didn't show up for work," said Danny. "Spencer, does any of this ring a bell? Any connections for you in Kosovo?"

Spencer thought for a moment, "No, none that I can think of. No previous operations, special forces, or agency involvement."

"It's a bit of a chase," said Abbasi, "but we know that some ethnic Muslims in the region were radicalized because of the atrocities Milosevic's men perpetrated on the Bosniaks and others during the war.

The U.S. didn't necessarily help when we occupied the country and allowed Saudi Arabia to funnel money to build mosques that taught Wahhabism. This led to a distorted version of the Quran and Islamic teachings. That, coupled with the anger from war and loss of life, is what fueled a majority of those radicalized. It's a shot in the dark, but it's possible."

Abbasi was all too familiar with the issues surrounding these two regions. Both times while assigned to the 10th Special Forces, he had served there: two separate deployments to Bosnia and Herzegovina in nineteen ninety-six when his team took over the Joint Commission Observer program from the British Army, and again in two-thousand and three when mass graves were found on Mount Crni Vrh. It was a vision that Abbasi still could not get out of his mind.

"Okay, but then, who do they work for?" asked Spencer. "Do you think Al Qaeda or Shahid-TB found their way to Kosovo? That wasn't the Amir's area of operation."

"True," said Abbasi, "but Spencer, going over your old case notes, you did mention a rumor that the Amir had been spotted in Kosovo at one time. No evidence was ever found to support the claim, but just because we did not find evidence doesn't mean it didn't happen."

Spencer had forgotten about this. There had been a claim from a foreign intel source that the Amir had been spotted in Pristina about a year before Spencer started with the Agency. Spencer had included it in his overall assessment in the case file to ensure all leads and sources were identified and reviewed. He considered that maybe Abbasi was right. Just because there was no evidence doesn't mean it didn't happen.

"You're right. I had forgotten about that lead. It came in before I was part of the agency, but I did review it. Nothing came of it. However, based on what we potentially have here, it may be worth looking at again."

Abbasi agreed. "I'll have my team start doing a thorough analysis on anything they can find that might connect the Amir to Kosovo."

"Oh, thanks for grabbing my bags from the Gasthaus yesterday," Spencer said to Abbasi. "I guess that's what you meant when you told your guys to bring an extra overnight bag?"

"I have a different overnight bag for you, Spencer. Finish your breakfast, and we'll deal with that," Danny said.

After breakfast, Gretta cleared the table. She knew the three men had other things to contend with. After a lifetime with Danny Doyle and the work he did, she had learned a thing or two about the necessity of the mission, and this one was personal to them both. Plus, Gretta was a little old-fashioned in her thinking about a wife's and a mother's responsibilities. It was how she was raised. She was a stay-at-home wife, not because her husband didn't want her to work; he was supportive and caring. He always gave her the choice to do whatever she wanted and supported her wishes and dreams one hundred percent of the time.

Contrary to the dangerously trained killer he could be, and often had to be, for his country, he had always been a gentle and loving husband at home. No, being a stay-at-home wife was her job to take care of the home and her husband. It was teamwork. She took care of him like he took care of her.

Gretta could never stand those loudmouthed women who yelled and screamed about women being able to do everything a man could do, or that all men were pigs. Gretta knew not all men were pigs, especially not hers. And as for being able to do everything a man could do, well, maybe there were a couple out there who could carry a hundred-pound rucksack through extreme heat or cold for thirty miles while avoiding detection or fighting their way to safety after being shot or injured, but she was sure the number was very few.

To Gretta, there was a difference between men and women; it was how they were designed. Their bodies were different, they thought differently, and physiologically and mentally, they were different in every regard.

She never saw that as something to complain about; it was something to celebrate. And everyone knew there were things that women could do (well, most women) that men never could.

Spencer and Abbasi stood up from the table and followed Danny outside through the back door of the kitchen. Once outside and down the stairs from the kitchen, Danny turned right along a concrete walkway.

Alongside the renovated old house was a wall constructed of concrete and painted white. The wall extended out from the house by about fifteen feet. Danny turned right at the end of the wall and headed toward the large driveway. The wall continued in that direction for another fifteen feet. Danny turned right again; the wall also made the same turn, but this time only about eight feet. Coming from the other side of the house was another wall, which would have overlapped the wall he was next to if there had not been a variance of approximately six feet between them. Spencer could see the wall had been constructed to hide what was inside its area.

It reminded him of the way they constructed vehicle lanes leading up to entry control points of military bases to keep suicide bombers from driving at full speed at the gate. This gave the gate guards time to react if the explosive detection machines they called "sniffers" detected any explosive residue on the vehicles driving through the maze of barriers.

Once the three men rounded the corner, Spencer saw where the second wall ended. There was a wooden gate with a padlock closing off the interior of the walled area. Danny took a set of keys out of his pocket and unlocked the gate. Once inside, he turned and locked the gate behind them. Spencer could see a large wooden door framed with a slightly pitched roof at its top. Painted white with a green roof, the door frame was approximately eight feet tall and four feet wide. The entire door, frame and all, was separated from the house. Danny took the keys from his pocket and unlocked the solid door. Once the door was opened, Spencer could see a steel door with what looked like a vault handle. To the right was a keypad and what he recognized as a biometric scanner.

"A bit overkill just to keep the neighbors out of your root cellar, don't you think, Danny?" Spencer said for a bit of levity, to which Abbasi smirked in acknowledgment of Spencer's comment.

“Maybe, but just wait till you see the rutabagas,” Danny replied, not looking back.

Danny then typed in a number on the keypad and placed his hand on the scanner. The sound of a mechanism disengaging could be heard from the metal door. Danny turned the vault handle and pulled the door open. The door was approximately seven feet by three feet, with three solid, round metal bar locking mechanisms running through the center of the door that secured it to the metal frame when locked.

A square staircase led from the vault door entrance towards the house by a few feet, then turned to the right and again leading down toward the back of the large driveway and the ‘L’ shaped shed area of the property.

At the bottom of the stairs was yet another metal door and a retinal scanner. Spencer thought to himself that there must be some hellacious produce down here.

Once Danny activated the retinal scanner and opened the remaining vault door, the three men walked into a bunker that was approximately thirty feet by sixty feet.

Spencer could see that there were cemented, structured rooms in parts of the space as well.

Along the side wall closest to the stairwell was a chain link cage with a metal door along the wall inside the cage. The section was about twenty feet long by fifteen feet wide. Lining the concrete wall were weapons racks. Some held M4s, a few SCARs, and a cornucopia of handguns mounted on pegs attached to the wall. On the opposite side of the cage were shelves of ammo cans and boxed ammunition: 5.56mm NATO rounds as well as 7.62mm for the SCARs. In addition, there were sections of handgun ammo: .45 Cal, 9mm, and others. There were other items in the cage as well—radios, earpieces, headsets, etc. A separate vault was also in the cage, which Spencer would learn held blasting caps, C4, pyrotechnics, fragmentation grenades, and 40mm launch grenades for the M203 that attached to the M4.

“What in the name of Double-0 Rambo is this?” Spencer said, more of a statement than a question.

“Welcome to my workshop,” said Danny.

"Glad this is only a hobby for you, Danny; I would hate to see what a full-time occupation would look like," mused Abbasi. "I like what you have done with the place."

"The facility is leftover from the Nazis; the decorations were purchased from a 'farm' in the States," Danny responded.

It was discovered a year after Danny and Gretta moved in. Danny was having the parking lot/driveway resurfaced and had to do underground inspections before digging or other work could begin. Since WWII items are valuable, Danny thought doing GPR (Ground Penetrating Radar) on the area might be a good idea.

What he found was a massive bunker that the Reich had built. The bunker was not on any plot maps of the property and he assumed it was unknown to the German government; local or federal. He decided to make the best of the discovery and made a few inquiries with the Agency, starting with Abbasi.

Danny suggested that, because of the size and location of the bunker, he might upgrade the underground facility and use it as an agency supply house for European operations. Weapons, communications devices, explosives, money, and other such items could be stored and issued as needed.

The CIA agreed and decided to supply engineers and workers from the Farm to do the work and ensure the secrecy of the operation by not using outside contractors.

Danny fielded questions from the surrounding neighbors by telling them that there was an uneven erosion of soil under the driveway. The German government was overburdened with regulations, so no one second-guessed his explanation.

The results were just a part of what Spencer and Abbasi saw before them now.

"I'm at a loss for words, for once," said Spencer.

"There's more to see. Follow me," said Danny. "Let me show you what Uncle Sam and Aunty CIA gave us."

Danny led them toward the right side of the bunker, where the group could see a large walled section with a door. Danny opened the door and walked in. As they entered the twenty-by-thirty-foot room, they found a nicely outfitted studio apartment. A well-made bed with a nightstand, lamp, and rug along the back side of the room. To the left was a small kitchenette with electric burners, a small electric oven, and a standard European-sized refrigerator. To the right was a small sofa and a comfortable chair facing the right wall, where a television and satellite box sat on a stand.

"And you had me staying at Frau Knopf's Gasthaus?" asked Spencer, acting as if his feelings had been hurt. "All you need is Wi-Fi down here."

"Built into the satellite cable system through a secure link from Langley. We get ESPN and satellite surveillance, all in one easy monthly plan," Danny replied in jest. "Come on, there's more to see."

Directly across the small hallway from the apartment room was a full bathroom: sink, shower, toilet, cabinet with towels and essentials.

"How does the toilet flush if we are about ten feet underground?" asked Abbasi. "Gravity typically works one way."

"A sump pump is used to push the waste upward into the main septic system," Danny explained. "This place uses water and electricity off the grid so as not to arouse suspicion when in use. Water is collected in a shed room through a catch system when it rains and also from a well on the property, using a filtration system to make it potable."

Next to the bathroom on the left side of the small hall was another room. Upon entering, Spencer and Abbasi could see shelves full of canned goods, dry goods, bottled water, shampoo, soap, etc.—enough to house someone for a couple of months, from the looks of it.

"Are you expecting a zombie apocalypse?" Spencer asked.

"With the upgraded air filtration system and heating and air conditioning, we could probably wait it out," was the reply.

"If need be, this is your fallback position, Spencer," Danny said, looking at Spencer.

"I'm not hiding, guys. I mean, I like my life and don't want to get murdered, same as the next guy. I'll take precautions and assist in finding this bastard, but I'm not hiding. It's yours and Gretta's fallback," Spencer responded.

"We can argue later, gentlemen," Abbasi spoke up. "For now, we have plans to make and a once-dead terrorist to find before he finds Spencer."

"Regardless of whether you choose to hide, you need access to the bunker," said Danny. He handed Spencer a keychain with a set of keys that were color-coded with key caps on the heads, except for one. "Yellow is for the padlock for the wooden gate; white is for the first door."

"What about the one that isn't color-coded?" asked Spencer.

"That's the house key," Danny said, looking at Spencer as if it were a silly question. "To be used anytime you want," he added.

It was his and Gretta's way of letting Spencer know he was welcome back into their home and their lives.

Spencer understood the gesture and could not respond for fear of getting choked up. He gave a slight nod toward his 'brother' with tightly pursed lips, attempting to keep his emotions in check.

"Next, we have to get your biometrics and retinal images scanned into the system," said Danny, walking around the corner of the small hallway.

At the back of the apartment wall was an open room with a couple of tables and desks. A laptop and monitors were on the desk, and a wall of smaller monitors were mounted above the desk. Each monitor showed a different area of the property. One showed the front door of the house; another showed the back door. One displayed an image of the house and driveway from what looked to be across the street from their property. Another showed two angles of the 'L'-shaped shed/stable area, and one was a top-down view of the walled-off section leading to the entrance of the bunker. There was a secondary set of monitors that showed the inside of the house: the kitchen, hallways, and living room.

Danny clicked the mouse attached to the laptop and pulled up a digital control panel. He clicked a button, and the screens changed to show street views leading to the house from all three streets. One even displayed the backside of the shed area up the street from the house.

"I have to admit, you thought of everything, Danny," said Abbasi.

"Maybe not," Spencer chimed in. "Lights, computers, air conditioning, and heat all require electricity. What happens during a power outage, or if someone cuts the power? You'll be in the dark down here."

"A backup generator ties into the main house electrical panel, which connects to the primary power supply for the bunker. However, there's also a backup wind and solar panel system on the shed with battery backups in case all power and the generator go out. Each system activates automatically should the other fail," Danny explained.

"I stand corrected," Spencer said, looking at Abbasi.

Danny turned on the biometric scanner to scan Spencer's handprint and entered it into the system. The system was separated from the main network as an 'on-premises' program to prevent hacking and unauthorized users from adding their prints from the user panel. Afterward, Danny used a portable iris scanner to add Spencer's retinal and iris scans for the last door.

"We are good to go. If Mr. Murphy wants to show his ugly mug around here, I think we've got it covered," Danny said, using the common nickname for when plans go awry and chaos ensues.

"Let's hope it doesn't happen, and we can find and kill this bastard before he finds us," said Spencer.

Chapter 9

Avni thought he was ready to do anything the Imam had asked of him, even death, if necessary.

Once the bomb went off yesterday at the place he worked, he changed his mind. Genuine fear struck him at the moment of the blast. He had thought he was up to the task, envisioning himself as an instrument of justice, as the Imam had taught him that his life was meant to bring retribution to the non-believers.

He had felt strong and fearless because that was how you felt when you were the one dealing out such carnage. But now, he felt fear. He realized he was not a hard man capable of handing out the sentence of death to others. He was weak, and as long as he was alive, he was okay with that.

Avni knew he had to get away from these people to whom he had pledged his loyalty. They did not care about him, only the means for him to carry out their ideas of revenge and justice. He had been so blind.

How could he have been so stupid and naïve as to let these people control his thoughts and actions? They had him believing he was doing the right thing. He now questioned everything the Imam had ever taught him. The idea of killing others because they did not believe in everything he believed was wrong. Avni now understood this. He was now one of them and questioned everything he thought he knew. The fear of death had changed him. Now, what was he to do?

Avni left work, along with many others from the hotel, yesterday. He returned to his apartment, scared of what would happen next. His roommate was off the work schedule for the next couple of days and was at the apartment. They discussed the blast and what they thought could have happened, although Avni was mostly aware of what had transpired.

The public was unaware of the specifics about the blast, and the authorities had not released information about it being a bomb. However, he knew the information he had given to his contact, Samir, at the protest had led to this bombing, but he dared not mention this to anyone.

Avni did not sleep much that night. He was afraid. He thought someone would be sent to kill him at home, or worse, ask him to take part in something much more insidious.

Avni got up early and packed only what he thought he needed to take with him. He was convinced he needed to be on the move until he could figure out what to do next. He would use his transportation card and ride the buses and trains all day until he knew what to do next. Better to stay on the move. No one could find him if he kept moving.

~~~

Goran walked up to the apartment building in Nuremberg's immigrant neighborhood. Not far from where he dropped off the backpack of explosives to the woman. The same woman who placed it in the hotel room of the man from the CIA who had hunted his father down in Tora Bora.

The woman was pleasant-looking enough for someone of her age. But his father was having his way with her now. He thought it was a waste of a loyal foot soldier in their mission, but his father explained they could not take any chances by leaving loose ends that could unravel their entire plan.

The younger one, the desk clerk at the hotel, was another loose end his father had told him about. Goran had gotten to know Avni only slightly at the Islamic center. Avni knew him as 'Samir,' an alias Goran had used to hide his true identity once he entered this country. He had obtained fake credentials: a German driver's license and a fake passport from Slovenia under the name 'Samir Kováč.'

The instructions from his father were to get rid of the boy, however he saw fit.
~~~

Goran did not have the same bloodthirst as his father seemed to enjoy. He preferred to make things quick and painless, if possible. He told himself his father never explicitly said to kill Avni, and he did say in whatever way Goran saw fit. But he also understood his father intended for him to take Avni's life and leave no trace or connection to him or his father.

He approached the door and knocked. The door opened, but it was not Avni.

"I need to speak to Avni," he said.

"He isn't here," replied the roommate, holding a bowl of cereal in one hand and the door with the other.

"Do you know when he will return?" asked Goran.

"No," was the half-interested reply from the young man standing in the doorway.

Goran could not leave and allow this person to identify him.

"Do you mind if I leave a note for Avni? I'm a friend from the Center," he continued.

The roommate opened the door wider to allow the man to enter and walked back inside the apartment, in front of the visitor, heading toward the kitchen area.

Goran quietly closed the door behind him, pulled a hunting-style knife from his waistband, and quickly walked up behind the roommate, who had his back to him. The young assassin swiftly brought his arm up and around the man's right shoulder and, with one quick, decisive move, brought the blade across his throat. He was graceful in his movements, quickly backing up during the kill to avoid blood splatter on his clothing.

The blue plastic cereal bowl, almost empty, fell to the floor with little noise, except for the spoon, which bounced for a moment off the floor, making a pinging sound as it hit. The remaining milk and cereal spilled across a small section of the floor, partially covered by the lifeless body, now mingling with blood pouring from the wound across the neck.

His body would eventually be found in a day or two at most. And if Avni found his roommate first, before the authorities, then he might take it as a sign to remain silent, at least until Goran had a chance to kill him as well.

He looked over the small apartment to see if he could find anything that would indicate where Avni had gone. What he found in Avni's room were a couple of empty drawers pulled open and a mostly empty wardrobe cabinet that only held the hotel uniform he would no longer need.

Goran assumed Avni was on the run and scared. He would look for the young man but figured he would be hard to find. No relatives in the city, and only his mother in Kosovo. He doubted Avni would head back there if he was frightened. The Imam had set him on this path, and he assumed Avni was smart enough to realize the connection the Imam had with this operation. He hoped for both their sakes that Avni would find a way to get far, far away and keep his mouth shut.

~~~

After making their way back up to the surface and securing the vault as they exited, Abbasi left the two men and made his way to the makeshift command center and contacted his team in Nuremberg for additional details.

His men had been scanning through days and hours of hotel security camera footage to look for any clues. A junior team member was combing through the system access records of the reservation logs.

Both teams uncovered interesting information.

The female suspect, Emina Begić, walked into the hotel hours before her shift was to start yesterday. A surveillance video showed her entering the front desk supervisor's office, carrying a backpack. The reservation software indicated that she accessed the record for room No. 560—John Spencer's room. The video also showed her leaving the office and taking the elevator to the 5th floor, where she entered room No. 560 with the backpack. She then left again without the backpack.

Additional records showed the desk clerk, Avni Shala, had also accessed records for room No. 560 the day before. There seemed to be a connection between the two, but they did not yet know what that connection was. Whatever it was, it involved Spencer and, Abbasi assumed, the Amir.

Abbasi instructed the team to trace these two individuals back to their origins and continue as long as necessary to find the connection.

~~~

Abu Sul–Malik walked back into the old office room in the warehouse, feeling refreshed and ready. He had taken time to have a small lunch and coffee with his son—a bowl of dahl, an Indian lentil soup, and roti, Indian bread. He felt relaxed and in good spirits.

Sitting in front of him, still tied to the chair, was Emina. She had challenged him and did not give up her screams easily. She was defiant. Unusual for a woman, and because of this, it made him work harder, and harder he did. Until finally, she relinquished the sweet release of agony with her screams of pain. Oh, what pleasure that brought him.

He had been frustrated at first, not getting his quick gratification from her. He felt denied. But when it finally came, the pleasure was so much sweeter. She had screamed so much that she could no longer make a sound. Now, he would partake in more physical pleasures of the flesh. Her will was so weakened that she could not fight. And then? Then, she would be a blank canvas on which to display his artistic abilities.

He would have to finish by tonight, he thought. He had other places to be in order to move his plan forward. But in the meantime, he would enjoy and savor every moment with the woman who was now laid out in front of him across the desk.

~~~

Abbasi stepped back into the house to inform Spencer and Danny of the update he had received.

For now, there was not much for them to do until actionable intel provided a direction. This was always the hardest part of the job, especially for men like them, who had trained and fought most of their lives. Sitting around waiting was more stressful and difficult than being in combat. All that pent-up energy and nothing to do with it.

They were not trained to stand by; they were trained to act. Even though they had all been out of the 'Teams' for several years now, and one was sitting behind a desk managing others or simply retired, they all had the same training and experience. They were men cut from the same cloth, and those tendencies didn't change, no matter how long you were out, regardless of what Spencer tried to tell himself.

"You happy with your kit, Spencer?" Abbasi asked him. By "kit," he was referring to Spencer's selection of weapons he had chosen from the bunker.
~~~

"The new FN 509 LS Edge is one hell of a handgun," Spencer said. "I'm surprised you have it already, Danny. It's the most customized off-the-shelf weapon on the market."

"It had better be the best. A team sniper designed it in collaboration with FN Herstal's American division, which is how I could get two first runs. The guy is one of the best and has a lot of combat field experience. He designed a weapon that met his specifications and included everything he couldn't find on the market."

"Versatility, speed, control, and accuracy," Spencer said, "everything a growing boy needs in a 9mm," he joked.

Spencer had also taken a tactical blade—curved, with a Kevlar sheath and a chain he could wear around his neck for quick use if needed. He also selected a braided wristband watch that hid a thin, flexible, serrated blade within the paracord braid. If he were captured and his hands were tied behind him, he had a way to cut free as long as they didn't take his watch. Spencer had also chosen a backup semi-auto he could use with an ankle holster: a Sig Sauer P365 Nitron Micro-Compact. Also a 9mm. Not as powerful as the .45 caliber, but just as deadly as long as you could put rounds on target. Spencer felt secure with his handgun selections. Now, to find that murderous bastard and use them.

~~~

Munich:

The man entered the hotel through the revolving doors at its entrance and walked straight through the lobby to the staff hallway leading to the kitchen. He was wearing coveralls with the company name "Munchener Schlusseldienst" (Munich Locksmith) on a patch over the left side.

He made his way to a single door just out of sight of the kitchen and used a bump key to unlock it. He then changed the lock, pulling out the industrial tumbler and lock set and replacing it with one from his toolbox. Once he screwed the base plate back onto the door, he tested the key to ensure it worked. It did. The man closed his toolbox, locked the door, placed the key in his pocket, and left the hotel.

This man did not speak the local language, but he knew you could gain access to almost any location as long as you looked and acted like you belonged there. How many people would stop a maintenance person
~~~

in a hotel to ask if they belonged there or what they were doing? Not even the hotel staff second-guessed his presence or what he was doing.

Chapter 10

Nuremberg:

8:00 pm. Salim Hassan, a well-dressed man in slacks and a sport coat, boarded the “ICE629” train to Munich at the Central Station on Bahnhofspl. in Nuremberg and sat in the four-seat first-class compartment. He had been in Nuremberg for the past couple of weeks on both business and, as of today, pleasure.

His work, for many years, had often been stressful and very political. It had, in fact, kept him running and on his toes for nearly three decades, and at one point, nearly killed him. Self-induced, he admitted, but he did love his work.

It was all the backstabbing and ambitious people who always wanted to make a name for themselves and take his place that annoyed him and drained most of the joy from his work. But he often knew of their ambitions and plans before they could carry them out, and he could assign them to dead-end assignments that took care of those ambitions.

Nearly a decade ago, he made the choice to set in motion a plan that would change his entire life and open up the world to him. No more stress, at least not anywhere near the level he had before. No job is perfect, after all. There was no more running, day in and day out. And no more looking over his shoulder.

He was a new man, free to pursue his wishes and desires without fears or concerns about hierarchy.

This trip to Germany, especially Nuremberg, had been personal—unfinished business of sorts—but it had not been without some unexpected and wonderfully gratifying rewards. He had not expected her to make him feel so good. He was still smiling, even now, while sitting on the train a few hours later. The man had spent time with many other women in his life, but she was something special. Such satisfaction she had given him. Yes, he thought, there were perks to what he did for a living.

His passport identified him as a Saudi citizen, sixty years old. Here in Europe on business, or so the European systems would verify. Of course, those records had been falsified, just as his passport had been.

Abu Sul-Malik had accomplished what he had come to Nuremberg to do. The man named John Spencer was dead. The man who had tracked him down in Tora Bora and allowed the infidels to track his whereabouts, or so they thought, until they took him out, or rather, his doppelganger.

Yes, the CIA agent was the catalyst for what had made him change his identity, altering the face he had been given when brought into the world. And the Amir could not let that stand. He had waited several years to get his revenge on all those who had taken part in Operation Grasshopper.

One such man had been an Afghan local who had betrayed his people by helping the American military and the CIA. There had been two of them, but only one had been found and dealt with. The other had fled his village, and no one knew where he had gone. Even torturing the tribe members in the village and killing the man's family had not produced information. He supposed they had truly been telling the truth. That was of no matter to him now.

The American military man named Morris had died before the Amir had the chance to get revenge. That was indeed sad news. A lost means to seek revenge, but Emina had helped make up for that loss; another smirk formed across his lips.

Her screams were not much different from those of others he had killed before, but her defiance at the beginning—refusing to give him her fear—was notable. Knowing the position she was in when he awakened her, she chose instead to be defiant. She had made him work for it. He had abused her in ways that, even now, made him blush. Her flesh provided him with so many different means of enjoyment. He had taken his desire both sexually and artistically.

He had brought her close to death a couple of times just to let her know he held her life in his hands, and only he could determine when she left this existence. Most of his followers believed that Allah was the only one who determined who lived and died, but he never actually believed that. Yes, she had made him work for her fear, and when she finally gave it, it produced such an overwhelming release of joy in him like he had not known since his first killing.

Now, only one man remained. Another traitor to his people. A man named Benham Abbasi, an Iranian turned infidel.

The man had fled his homeland to become an American soldier and spy.

The Amir had learned that Benham Abbasi had left the military and joined the CIA. He had been one of the three American men who had tracked him down in Tora Bora, and now he had to pay with his life.

His sources in America had tracked the man down in Virginia and followed him to Germany. They were under strict orders not to kill him. That particular satisfaction would belong to him and him alone. They had followed him to Munich and lost him at the airport. Now that he had dealt with John Spencer, he was on his way to Munich to find this man.

The Amir's plan was to draw the man out of hiding. He would cause an event that would surely bring this man out of his hiding place to investigate. Then, the Amir and his men would be watching the area, looking for this apostate and tracking him from there until the Amir could seize the moment and take him out.

The Amir's men had built a small network of loyalists in the city. Of course, none of them knew it was Abu Sul-Malik, as he was supposed to be dead, but loyal to the cause nonetheless.

There was a large Muslim community here, especially around the central station area of the city. There were over one hundred thousand Muslims in this capital city of Bavaria, most of whom were immigrants from Syria, Iraq, and Afghanistan. And, with Munich being a very conservative Christian city, there was an impact on Muslims living there.

Mosques had been closed by the government or forced out by property owners. Many of the people who owned buildings in the city refused to rent to Muslims for fear of a mosque in their community, and many didn't want Muslim immigrants in their neighborhoods. Many remembered the issues with the Turks who had migrated to Germany decades earlier and were still bitter about it. They were not looking to have a repeat. But the German government had forced its hand. Citizens had been compelled to open their homes and spare rooms to house these immigrants, and the people were angry.

Crackdowns led to fewer and fewer places where Muslims could pray, which led to anger and resentment within the Muslim community; exactly what Abu Sul-Malik had looked for. He could use this to his advantage, especially with the younger generation and even some of the older ones.

Christians against Muslims: an age-old problem. Another Crusade could help level the playing field, thought the terrorist.

~~~

Avni got off the bus at the central station in Nuremberg. He had decided to leave the city and head south to Munich, another large city where he could find work. He needed to get out of Nuremberg and away from the people that had led him to partake in the actions that caused not only the deaths of those he had considered non-believers but also had almost gotten him killed as well.

Thinking about what had transpired since yesterday made him paranoid. And he thought, for good reason. He was convinced they would be looking for him once they realized he had fled the city. But he couldn't just wait around for them to kill him. He couldn't continue to support the death of the innocent. He had been taught most of his life to hate non-believers, that they were nothing more than filthy infidels who deserved a just punishment of death.

Avni now understood how wrong they and he had been. Maybe he had known this all along, but he was so full of anger that he allowed himself to be drawn in by these people who had used him to their advantage at his own risk.

He hoped the community in Munich would be better. He had nothing except for what he was carrying. But he felt better knowing he was getting away from those looking for him in Nuremberg.
~~~

Avni boarded train number “ICE629” at the Central Station, headed to Bavaria's capital. The train would continue on to Prague, but Avni only needed to go as far as Munich. He used his bank card to purchase the ticket on his phone while traveling on the bus to the Central Bahnhof.

Avni was sitting in the second-class section of the train but felt somewhat exposed. Still fearful of being found, he sat in his seat, looking out the window and turning every time the door to his train opened.

After the train had pulled away from the station and was underway, Avni felt hungry. His stomach growled, as he hadn’t eaten since yesterday. The adrenaline of yesterday’s events and the fear of being killed had gotten the better of him. He had been traveling all day on trams and buses and had not stopped to eat. There was a meal car on this train, and he decided to make his way through a couple of compartments to get a sandwich and hot tea.

Walking through the train, Avni kept his eyes open just to be safe. Passing the private compartments, he noticed a man sitting alone. The man was dressed in slacks and a sport coat and appeared to be of Arab descent. The man looked up and saw Avni. Their eyes met for a moment. The man smiled at Avni and nodded his head. Avni smiled back and continued to the meal car.

~~~

How fortunate, thought Abu Sul-Malik, Allah continues to bless… well, me. Not so much the young Avni.

The Amir recognized the young man who had just walked past his compartment as the clerk at the Le Méridien hotel. The same young man he had just instructed his son, Goran, to dispose of. It appeared the young man had gotten away. Well, thought Abu, ‘Away from the Spider, and into the web.’

The Amir considered killing the boy on the train. Cutting his throat would be fairly easy. He was but a child; skinny and weak, judging by his appearance. Of course, poverty and a lack of food have a way of doing that to a person. However, slicing a person’s throat is very messy; too much blood. The chances of the body being discovered before he got off the train were high, and the train conductor would report it to the authorities, and the ‘Polizei’ would interview everyone on the train before letting them leave. He neither had the time nor patience to take that risk.
~~~

The Amir decided to use a different tactic with the young man and see where that would lead. Avni did not know the Amir. He had only interacted with Goran and the imam in Kosovo, who taught and recruited Avni, per the Amir's request for this mission, as he did the others who were recruited from the Madrasa.

Abu Sul-Malik stood up and walked out of his first-class compartment and into the meal car, where he found Avni sitting at a table sipping a cup of hot tea. There were not many people on the train this evening, so there was little chance of being disturbed.

"As-Salaam-Alaikum," he said to Avni as he walked in and saw the young man sitting there.

"Wa-Alaikum-Salaam," Avni responded, guarded but feeling the necessity to answer the greeting. "Are you Muslim?" Avni asked.

"I am," said Abu, as if there were no other options. "And you?"

"Yes," Avni replied, still unsure of the stranger.

"My name is Salim. Salim Hassan," the Amir said, placing his hand over his heart with the slightest nod of his head toward Avni to indicate his warm and peaceful intentions toward the young man.

"Avni. Nice to meet you, Mr. Hassan."

"Would you like to join me for a meal?" the Amir asked.

"Thank you, but unfortunately, I only have enough for tea," Avni replied, embarrassed by his situation and meager means.

"Then you must let me buy you dinner," said the Amir with a smile.

"Thank you, sir, that's very kind of you, but really, it's unnecessary."

"The Qur'an says, 'The righteous are those who give food in spite of love for it to the needy, the orphan, and the captive; we feed you only for the countenance of Allah.'" was the Amir's response. He looked at Avni with a smile and a questioning expression, motioning toward the counter.

"Thank you," said Avni, accepting the man's offer. He almost felt guilty at his suspicion of this man's charity toward him. He quoted the Qur'an regarding charity, not hate. Mr. Hassan was only trying to be a good Muslim according to his faith, and Avni repaid his kindness with suspicion.

The two ordered their meals and sat at the table together.

"So, where are you from, Avni?"

"Kosovo. I came to Germany for work."

“Are you heading to Prague?” was the next question.

“No, sir,” Avni replied. “I’m going to Munich to find work.”

“And what kind of work do you do?” asked the Amir.

“Hotel clerk, restaurant, office. Anything that will pay enough for me to cover rent and food,” said the twenty-two-year-old.

“I think I can help you with that,” the Amir replied, dangling the carrot.

“Really? How?” was Avni's surprised response.

“I own a restaurant in Munich, next to a delightful hotel. I also know the managers of the hotel if you prefer to work there. I have several friends in Munich who can help.” The Amir was confident he had now gained the boy's trust.

This was wonderful, thought Avni. Maybe Allah is smiling upon me. Here I am, running for my life, trying to escape those who lured me into this terrible way of life, and now, praise Allah, He has placed this man on my train to help me.

“Thank you, Mr. Hassan. You are a kind and decent man,” Avni said to the man seated across from him, oblivious to the truth about Abu Sul-Malik.

After dinner, the Amir asked Avni if he would prefer to sit in his private compartment for the rest of the journey to Munich. The Amir graciously offered this more to keep an eye on the boy than as an attempt at hospitality, to which Avni gratefully accepted. Once in the train compartment, Abu Sul-Malik made sure Avni was ‘comfortable’ and excused himself to make a couple of phone calls on Avni’s behalf to let his friends look for opportunities. Avni could not believe his luck, nor could the Amir.

Chapter 11

Charley Hall was raised in the farm belt of Ohio, in Lewisburg, a small town few had ever heard of unless they were from there.

Long country roads lined with corn fields and soybean crops stretched as far as the eye could see.

The community consisted of solid Christian families mixed with the German Brethren, a group similar in some ways to the Amish. His father had been an aircraft mechanic during the Korean War and was determined to become a farmer once the war ended.

Charley's father was the hardest-working man he had ever known, rising before sunrise every day to handle the chores for the chickens, cows, and pigs—all before he started working the fields.

When Charley was old enough to help, his father taught him to milk the cows and feed the chickens and hogs, instilling in Charley the meaning of responsibility and work ethic.

Charley's mother was a kind woman, supportive of her husband and son. She cooked breakfast and dinner and cared for the home. She was also the treasurer of the local school district. His mother held the family together, even their extended family; she was the glue binding what was a widely dispersed family on both sides.

Education was of great importance to his parents. His mother held a degree in finance from what had been a women's college in the nineteen-fifties. She would sit with him every night after cleaning up from supper and go over his homework with him. She would tutor him on the rare occasions he needed help with math, but Charley seemed to excel in all his classes. Throughout high school, he would wake up early with his father, do his chores on the farm, and prepare for school.

Charley graduated high school with a four-point-zero grade point average while still finding time to compete in track. He even managed to take second place in the state competition one year. Charley had wanted to play football but worried that if he got injured, it would prevent him from helping his father on the farm, which he couldn't risk. Charley idolized his father and was grateful for the hard work his dad did for him, his mother, and their community. His father always found time to help others in need.

Charley attended Ohio State University on a combination of academic and sports scholarships. His parents were people of humble means, and Charley was determined to help pay his own way through college. He earned his degree in history and political science to prepare for law school. Before graduating, he applied and was accepted to George Mason Law School.

During law school, he continued his academic achievements, determined to make his parents proud; then 9/11 happened. Charley felt a strong urge to do something to help his country, but he didn't know what. He considered the military but was determined to finish law school first. Two years into law school, he was approached by a man who spoke to him privately about a potential career in the CIA.

The man seemed to understand Charley's desire to contribute to the safety of his country and its citizens.

After a few interviews, psychological evaluations, and physical assessments, Charley decided to leave law school and join the CIA.

Now, he was one of Behnam Abbasi's dedicated field agents. Currently in Nuremberg, he had been coordinating with the Bundesnachrichtendienst, the German Federal Intelligence Service. The BND, as it was known, was the German counterpart to the CIA. Abbasi had stopped in Munich upon arriving in Germany to coordinate efforts with the BND to use their facial recognition and camera surveillance systems, hoping to catch the terrorist known as the Amir. Now, Agent Hall was using it to identify and track the two suspects in the bombing.

The facial recognition software had been under development for the past twenty years.

Currently, there were lawsuits against the state for illegally using the software during an international summit a few years ago.

Regardless of the legal standing, the head of the Federal Police Force, in cooperation with the heads of the BND and MAD, Germany's Military Counterintelligence Service, had all agreed to implement and discreetly run the application in a joint surveillance center.

The center was known to very few within the political structure to ensure it was not publicized for political activities and to keep the public from knowing of its application.

The surveillance center combined the facial recognition systems with the camera systems of train stations, taxis, trains, sidewalks, streets, and business cameras.

All of these camera systems were tied into the government's data system and could transmit directly to the center, or specific cameras could be accessed where video could be reviewed up to two weeks prior.

Pictures from the hotel employee records were uploaded for both Emina and Avni, and a search was run within the facial recognition system. Each person returned hundreds of hits within a two-week timeframe. The surveillance system provided an accuracy readout for each hit. From there, the team could sort by parameters. This time, they selected hits that were accurate to eighty-five percent or above. Still, there were dozens of hits for each of the two suspects.

Charley started with the dates of the blast and identified both suspects. The woman, identified as Emina Begić, was noted to have entered the hotel several hours before her scheduled shift, carrying a backpack that the team had already assessed was used to carry the explosive device into the hotel. Surveillance also captured her leaving the hotel.

Likewise, the software detected Avni Shala entering the hotel twelve minutes and thirty-seven seconds before his shift started and showed him working the front desk and assisting guests during the time before the blast. It later showed him in the street with other employees and guests after the blast, then leaving prior to people being allowed back into the hotel.

A search of the reservation system showed Emina Begić accessing the records of John Spencer the morning she planted the bomb and showed Avni accessing the same record two days prior.

Currently, Charley had personnel in the surveillance center looking into Avni's whereabouts the day before he accessed the reservation records and after leaving the hotel, as well as Emina's whereabouts during the same timeframe.

Agent Hall hoped this would potentially identify other people of interest in the bombing they could track down and eventually lead them to the primary target of their investigation.

A team had been dispatched to each of the two suspects' addresses on file. A man who appeared to be Avni Shala's roommate had been found murdered in their apartment, with his throat cut. Surveillance footage showed Avni leaving early that morning with a backpack. Video showed the young man checking around corners and repeatedly looking behind him to see if he was being followed.

That was very suspicious behavior. Did he help plant the bomb and kill his roommate? Agent Hall wondered.

The cameras also detected another man in his mid-twenties entering the building earlier that morning for about ten minutes, then leaving again. His face did not match any of the known occupants of the building, and although that was not enough to imply guilt, the timing coincided with the time of death of the roommate, making it sufficient grounds to run a search and investigate the man. Maybe Avni Shala hadn't killed his roommate, but that didn't clear him of involvement in the bombing.

The apartment looked normal except for Avni's room. His clothes had been taken, and drawers were left open while hangers were emptied, except for his hotel uniform. The kid was on the run. The team surmised that the backpack he was carrying in the video contained his personal belongings rather than another explosive device, but they couldn't be sure. Was it the blast that scared him? Was he running from someone? Charley's gut feeling, along with the fact that Avni had researched John Spencer's details in the hotel registry system, indicated that the kid was involved; but how, he wasn't sure. The team continued its surveillance to track Avni.

BND had also tracked Emina Begić's movements after the blast. Her apartment didn't turn up any new clues. However, the 'Sniffer', as it was referred to, was a hand-held explosive vapor detector that had picked up trace elements of the explosives used in the blast at the Le Meridien. They knew the bomb had been in the apartment. Who was this woman, and why was she planting devices to kill a former agency operative? Was she working with the Amir, or was this something different?

The German team monitoring the surveillance footage picked up Emina leaving the apartment, taking a bus to the south side of the city, and walking to an abandoned warehouse. There was no evidence of her leaving the warehouse, but they did get a glimpse of a man exiting.

~~~

CIA and BND dispatched a joint team to the warehouse located between Frankenstrasse and Katzwangerstrasse and entered the overgrown parking lot with weapons in hand.

The Germans wore dark tactical clothing and balaclavas to conceal their identities.

Most of the BND agents worked undercover on several counterintelligence operations and could not risk their identities being discovered.

Once inside the warehouse, the teams spread out to canvas both floors of the empty space.

Shortly after entering, Charley was helping to clear the ground floor when he heard one of the BND agents announce over their earpiece comms that they had found something on the second floor.

Charley grabbed the grimy, paint-chipped rails of the metal grate staircase and made his way up to the second floor. He walked forward to the room where a couple of BND agents were standing.

Nothing he had ever done at the Farm prepared him for what he saw when he entered the office. Charley's face turned pale, and he felt his heartbeat speed up. His ears muffled the sounds around him. He almost fell as his body reacted to the horrifying scene faster than his mind could comprehend.

Splayed across the desk was the woman named Emina Begić. Naked, her clothes were in shreds on the floor. Blood was everywhere; some areas of the room looked more like a Jackson Pollock painting than a
~~~

murder scene. Blood spatter went across the floor to the walls and from the walls to the ceiling, almost as if someone had taken a paintbrush and deliberately applied it that way.

The woman was on her back, sprawled across the desk. Her legs draped over the outer edge of the desk and were spread apart, while her arms were outstretched over each side. Strips of what looked like telephone cord had secured both her arms and legs in place. Her eyes were open, empty black sockets, as was her mouth. Her eyes were missing, and her eyelids had been removed, in what could only have been an attempt to keep the victim from closing her eyes and forcing her to witness what was being done to her. The woman's head was turned, facing the edge of the desk.

Charley Hall shook his head in an effort to dispel the thought and image that plagued him. He felt sickened just by the thought of what he was imagining had taken place here, and he prayed he was wrong. He would have to go to confession at some point to deal with the thoughts that had entered his psyche. No man or monster could be capable of such an act as what had invaded his mind.

A couple of members of the BND team were assigned to photograph the scene and collect fingerprints and blood samples. Fingerprints would be crucial if any could be found of the monster who had committed this unimaginable act. A full canvassing of the warehouse and surrounding area would have to be done to find evidence, if it existed. That might take the team days to complete.

Charley walked out of the room and into the parking lot area, sick to his stomach. He pulled out his cellphone and called Behnam Abbasi.

~~~

Abbasi hung up the phone, somewhat shocked by the imagery Agent Hall had described to him regarding the scene. Hall had given him a thorough rundown of the information they had gathered so far in searching the apartments, the dead roommate, and the ongoing video footage they were reviewing to find Avni Shala. Charley would keep him apprised of any developments he and the BND uncovered.

Abbasi walked toward the house to update Spencer and Danny about what he had learned so far. Due to the violent nature of the information, he did not want Gretta to hear. Not that Gretta wasn't strong enough to
~~~

handle the news and subject matter, but rather because it was hard enough for him, and he was a seasoned and callused warrior and agent. He would let Danny decide whether to inform his wife if he felt it prudent to do so.

One thing confused Abbasi. He didn't remember the Amir being so malicious or gruesome with his victims before. Was this the Amir? Maybe a henchman who was a bloodthirsty lunatic? Was the woman's death even related to the Amir? It seemed unlikely to be a random act or the work of a serial killer. This type of killing was ritualistic in its approach, and from what Agent Hall told him—and based on the video footage—she had gone there deliberately, most likely to meet the person who murdered her. It stood to reason that her murder was tied to the bombing.

He walked through the back door and into the kitchen. Danny and Spencer had been going over old case files of the Amir to see if anything jogged Spencer's memory or if something new jumped out at them that he had missed years ago. Abbasi had included updated notes he and his team had gathered over the past few months in case something tied into what they were learning now.

"Jesus!" said Spencer after Abbasi had filled them in on the call with Agent Hall.

"Looks like they are tying up loose ends with anyone involved," Danny responded.

"We suspected as much, but we still haven't tracked down the kid Avni yet. We don't know if he is alive or dead," said Abbasi.

"What's in the warehouse area where the woman was killed? Why there, specifically?" asked Spencer.

"We don't know yet," said Abbasi, "but I assume it might be because it's in a loud industrial area of the city and a large, abandoned factory warehouse. No prying eyes. You probably couldn't hear the screams due to all the loud machinery and the enormous distances between buildings."

Abbasi walked over to the counter where their hosts kept the alcohol. He grabbed a bottle of the good stuff that Danny seemed to prefer—Lagavulin 16-year-old Scotch. It was too early in the day to be drinking, but if there were ever a reason for exceptions, he assumed this was one.

Abbasi didn't even stop to ask if it was okay. The visions of what Charley described were horrific, no matter who you were or what you had done or seen in war; this was sickening. He grabbed a small glass from the cupboard and started pouring himself a drink. Danny told him to bring two more glasses and the bottle.

The three of them sat there for the next thirty minutes, sipping on their scotch and trying to focus on the case files in silence. There wasn't much they could say or discuss about those details.

Abbasi's phone rang. He looked at the caller ID; it was Agent Hall. "Go," he answered.

"We've hit pay dirt," said Charley on the other end. "We found a bloody fingerprint under the left inside thigh—actually, a thumbprint. It appears he tried to wipe off the fingerprints and missed this one. No other prints were found on the body. The placement shows he was standing between her legs at the time the print was made, as if spreading her legs apart or gripping her thighs," said the more junior CIA officer.

"Evil animal" was Abbasi's initial response. "Any hits in IAFIS?" was his next question.

AFIS was the Automatic Fingerprint Identification System run by Interpol, and IAFIS was the integrated system maintained by the FBI.

It housed the fingerprints and histories of seventy million subjects, thirty-one million of which were civil prints, and the prints of about seventy-three thousand known and suspected terrorists, including The Amir.

"Yes!" said Charley. "And it's a doozy."

"Are you sure?" Abbasi asked intensely. "We have to be certain."

"The match was ninety-eight percent," confirmed Agent Hall.

"Did you get visual confirmation?" he asked.

"That's the weird thing," Hall said. "We captured an image of a man leaving the scene, but it was definitely not The Amir."

"Stay on it and let me know what else you find."

"There's more," Hall said quickly, before Abbasi could hang up.

"What else you got?"

"The kid, Avni. The Germans were able to track him throughout the day. He jumped from one bus to a tram and onto another bus to the Bahnhof. The kid was on the move all day. The video shows him looking around every corner as he made his way, searching for anyone following him. He finally departed the central station with a ticket he purchased online before getting to the station. He boarded an 8 p.m. train to Munich last night."

"What's in Munich?" Abbasi inquired.

"Unknown," said his subordinate. "Maybe he's just on the run."

"Keep me posted." And Abbasi hung up.

Time to update the guys for the second time in less than an hour.

Chapter 12

Avni awoke, feeling sore and with his eyes swollen from crying. The night had not been a pleasant one.

He and Salim had arrived at the central station and were greeted by two of Salim's men. Salim had told him the men were his drivers.

The four men walked around the corner to the Parkplatz to a black Mercedes Benz Sprinter van with no windows.

Salim had told him that he would provide Avni with a room until he could interview for the job he had set up for Avni tomorrow. For now, he would be given a warm place to sleep, safe and comfortable for the night.

As Avni was climbing into the side door of the van, Salim pulled out the stun gun from his bag and zapped Avni in the back of the head, just as he had done to the woman at the warehouse. Avni fell face down, with his head between the seats and slumped across the sidestep of the van. The two men bound his hands and feet behind him and gagged him. Then they placed him on the seat behind where their boss would be sitting.

Avni came to as they were dragging him into a dimly lit room that had a single light fixture with one exposed bulb hanging from the ceiling, barely bright enough to see.

The walls were cement and had no windows. It felt like being in a tomb: cold and dark. As he was tossed against the wall, still tied and gagged, he could see a drain in the floor in the center of the room. The door closed behind the men as they exited. It was a solid wooden door, and Avni could hear the deadbolt being locked, sealing him to his fate. His luck had indeed run out.

He was left there all night, bound, cold, and wrapped in fear; to pray, to cry, to lose hope, to think of a way to escape, to lose hope again, and then become frantic. Crying, thrashing against the restraints on his arms and ankles, he pissed himself because of a combination of extreme fear and a full bladder.

Of course, Abu Sul-Malik had a front-row seat and watched this from the video camera installed in the room. Or, at least, he watched until he felt the need to go to bed. He had to get a good night's sleep. After all, he had work to do tomorrow.

~~~

The Amir finished watching the video of the boy squirming in fear throughout the night as he ate his breakfast the following morning. He wanted nothing more than to indulge in his sinister deeds as he had with the woman in Nuremberg. But he thought he had given this assignment to his son. He needed to send a message to Goran and have him come to Munich. He would finish his assignment after explaining how the boy got away. For Goran's sake, he had better be willing to finish the job. His offspring was a means to an end; he could not risk any loose ends, regardless of who that loose end might be. If Goran chose to kill the boy, so be it. If he did not, Goran would die. It made no difference to him, either way.

Abu Sul-Malik was staying in an old country house that had once been used as a Gasthaus. It was twenty-two kilometers south of the city and on the edge of the town of Feldkirchen-Westerham. Close enough to Munich but far enough away so as not to draw suspicion. It was owned by a shell corporation that could not be easily traced but was essentially owned by members of Al-Qaeda.

Salim Hassan was checked into, of all places, the Le Méridien down the street from the central train station. He found this somewhat humorous. The house was less than 45 minutes from the hotel and central station.

The Amir gave instructions for one of his men to get word to his son to meet him at his hotel today.

~~~

Goran's phone rang. The voice on the other end gave the code name and address to a location in Munich and explained that his presence was required urgently.

Goran understood the message. His father wanted to see him immediately, and he would need to get to the hotel in Munich as quickly as possible.

Goran looked up at the Munich station and the hotel and realized he could walk from the station within minutes. He grabbed an overnight bag and a gun and left his room, heading toward Bahnhofstrasse to catch the train to Munich.

~~~

It was late in the afternoon, and Agent Charley Hall was back at the central command of the BND Surveillance Center. The BND agents returned to him with a couple of new pieces of very important information.

They had tracked the man from the apartment building where the dead roommate of Avni Shala had been found. They could follow his trail to a Gasthaus where he had entered and had not left.

A team was headed there now to investigate and find out who the man was.

Second, they had tracked the man leaving the warehouse and followed him to a car, which was traced back to a rental company. The car had been rented to a 'Salim Hassan' of Saudi Arabia. The picture did not look like the Amir at all. They followed the vehicle to a hotel very near the Central Station, off of Bahnhofsplatz and Königstor, called the Hotel Victoria. He checked out of the hotel yesterday and took the ICE629 to Munich.

Agent Hall realized this was the same train the boy, Avni, had boarded at the same time last night.

"Send a team to that hotel and find out which room this man stayed in and hope to God they haven't cleaned the room yet!" he ordered. "We need to go over that room with a fine-tooth comb. I need fingerprints, DNA, or anything else that may have been left behind. We need to identify this man immediately."

Agent Hall picked up the phone and called Abbasi. At this rate, he should put his boss on speed dial, he thought.
~~~

~~~

Abbasi answered the phone. “Go.”

“Details are coming in fast. BND was able to track the man leaving the warehouse from where the woman was murdered,” Agent Hall continued to think of the victim as ‘the woman’ instead of by her name, so as not to personalize the evil that had been done to her. Regardless of her part in the bombing, it helped him cope with the imagery by not humanizing her to that extent.

“The man was identified as a Saudi national named Salim Hassan. Video footage showed him getting into a rental car and tracked him to the Hotel Victoria, not far from the central station here in Nuremberg.”

“Close enough to jump on the first train out of town to make a getaway if needed,” was his boss’s reply.

“Already done,” said the agent. “He boarded a train to Munich last night, five minutes before Avni Shala boarded. Bnd has a team headed to the hotel to look for any evidence. BND also has a team handling surveillance video in real time in Munich, looking for both suspects. We also managed to track down the man exiting Avni Shala's apartment after the murder of his roommate. He is staying at a Gasthaus in the city. We have another team on the way there to look for and question him.”

“I think we might be heading to Munich,” said Abbasi. And with that, he hung up and looked at the two men sitting across from him. “Grab your bags. Munich looks like the next hot spot.”

“But it’s not even October yet,” quipped Spencer.

“Yeah, but I’m sure we can find you a Fräulein to keep you busy,” said Danny. “Or, at least, a bratwurst.”

The group needed a laugh. Spencer and Danny used to make jokes as a way to cope with the impending seriousness of dangerous operations. Men in their line of work typically found unusual means by which to cope with danger and death.

Some used inappropriate humor, some meditated, and some used alcohol or working out. Sarcasm and alcohol had been theirs. And for Danny, the support of his wife, Gretta, backed it up. That woman was a rock, thought Danny. The fear of losing her was almost too much for him to think about. He was thankful for her recovery. He would do anything for her.
~~~

~~~

The BND team sent to the Gasthaus to find the man from the video at the apartment entered. They showed the woman in charge a picture of the man they suspected of killing Avni's roommate and asked if she had seen him.

"Yes," said the woman, "Samir."

She described him as a very nice young man. He had been there for almost two weeks, renting a room. She had just seen him leave a little while ago, but she did not know where he was going, and she had not asked.

The team entered his room and searched for anything that might help in their investigation. What they found was a notepad sitting on the desk in the room. Using an old investigator's trick of shadowing the indentations from what had been written on the sheet above it with a pencil, they uncovered the following message:

'Le Méridien'–Babi Bayerstrasse 41, Munich, room #614.

They also took fingerprints and hair samples from a brush and a toothbrush in the bathroom to conduct DNA testing.

~~~

Another BND team was at the Hotel Victoria.

The German agents spoke to the manager on duty and showed him a picture of the man from the warehouse. This team used the passport photo of the person in question to show to the manager. The manager confirmed that the person was checked into the hotel.

What room was he staying in?

The manager looked up Salim Hassan's name and provided them with his room number. Housekeeping was possibly in the room now.

The manager took them up the elevator to the man's room on the third floor. Housekeeping was already in the room and had started with the bed linens. The team forced the manager and housekeeping out of the room and conducted a sweep for explosives. Luckily, none were found.

The team went through the trash, looked for hair samples from the bed, and fingerprints from the shower door handle, sink, desk, remote control for the TV, and telephone. They collected every piece of evidence they could find to process and returned to the command center after verifying the man had checked out.

~~~

As Abbasi briefed his men at the house and prepared for most of them to accompany him to Munich, Danny was saying goodbye to Gretta while grabbing a seventy-two-hour bug-out bag he kept packed for emergencies.

A 'bug-out bag' was a tactical backpack with enough changes of socks and underwear, a couple of t-shirts, calorie food bars, and water, as well as other tactical necessities for seventy-two hours.

Danny had additional items in his bag, including a plasma lighter, high-strength paracord, a folding blade, a baseball cap, and cash.

Gretta knew there was nothing she could say to change his mind, and she didn't want to try. He had given up his life to move here with her when she was sick so she could be closer to home. They both wanted to help protect Spencer. So, all she could say to the man she had been married to for most of her life and loved with all her heart was, "Be careful and come back to me alive."

Danny stooped and kissed his wife gently and lovingly. "Ich liebe dich, mein Schatz," which in English translates to "I love you, sweetheart." Danny was never very good at speaking German, but he did learn that phrase and learned it well.

Spencer went to his room and packed his medium-sized backpack with clothes, a laptop, and ammo. He kept both guns and the knife on his person until this was over. He was having a hard time understanding how the Amir was still alive, let alone in Germany, and that no one, not even the authorities, had noticed him. Was he no longer on any watchlist? Did the algorithms of the facial recognition software fail to identify him because he was supposed to be dead? As far as Spencer knew, they left those images in the databases for just such crazy situations. How had he not been identified yet? He grabbed his bag and went downstairs.

Behnam's men had pulled the van to the side entrance of the vault and were loading a rifle rack with M4s and a couple of MP5s with ammo. They were also loading a container of comms equipment and bulletproof vests. Spencer realized this was going to get serious very fast.

He was hoping for a quick end to this insanity and found himself wishing for little to no civilian casualties. But he knew, historically, that was not the most likely outcome.
~~~

Danny and Gretta were standing by the Audi Q7 crossover that he and Abbasi had arrived in from Nuremberg.

Spencer threw his pack in the back and walked over to them.

"Be careful and take care of each other," Gretta said, looking at Spencer and then Danny.

"I will bring him back; you have my word," said Spencer. She reached up and gave Spencer a hug, touching his face with both hands, as a mother would do to a son. Spencer smiled and walked to the other side of the Audi to give them a moment alone.

About the same time, Abbasi walked up and looked at Danny. "Time to go." Abbasi turned to Gretta and said, "I am leaving two men here to look after you and coordinate with my team in Nuremberg. They will take shifts throughout the night, watching the house. Anything you need, just let them know."

With that, he walked to the passenger side of the car.

Danny hugged his wife and gave her a kiss. "See you soon," he said and climbed into the back seat.

Gretta stood in the driveway as she watched the vehicles pull out of sight. She had a sickening feeling in her stomach.

Chapter 13

Agent Hall had the BND lab run the DNA tests again. There had to be a mistake, and he sure as hell was not going back to Abbasi with a screwed-up result when things were this important.

The fingerprints from the hotel came back as those of Abu-Sul-Malik, as did the DNA from the small hairs pulled from the bed linens. That was good news. However, the DNA from the toothbrush and hair samples at the Gasthaus of the murder suspect Avni Shala's roommate came back as a match to the Amir as well.

These results had to be a mistake. The Amir was of Middle Eastern descent, and the man 'Goran' they were looking for was from Kosovo. According to the DNA results, they were supposed to be related.

Hall's phone beeped with an incoming text. DNA tests had been re-run, and the results were in. There was a ninety-three percent match between the two samples. The younger suspect was a match to Abu Sul-Malik, and the man's DNA in the hotel room was a match to the Amir as well, but the man in the video was not the Amir. They looked nothing alike. Could the man be another relative? A brother or a cousin?

Agent Hall picked up the phone to call Abbasi.

~~~

The vehicles had been on the road for about forty-five minutes, headed to Munich on the A9 Autobahn.

The drive had been quiet and somber thus far.
~~~

Spencer was in his own head, thinking about a multitude of things: his friends risking themselves for him after all these years, and his abandoning them years ago and not being there when they needed him most. He was also thinking about Abbasi, and how well this job seemed to fit him, not to mention his taking such a personal interest in helping Spencer.

He was also reflecting on his life to this point, as well as other demons that seemed to creep into his thoughts during moments of deep self-reflection. 'Woulda, coulda, shoulda.'

Would they find the Amir? Could they catch him and his minions before anyone else got hurt? Should they take all of them out to ensure they didn't get the chance to do it again?

Abbasi's phone rang. "What's the latest?" he asked, answering the phone.

"I hope you are sitting down," Agent Hall said.

"Hold on, I'm putting you on speaker," Abbasi replied.

"Then I hope you are all sitting down," Hall responded, his tone lacking humor and tinged with nervousness.

"The kid we tracked down who killed Avni Shala's roommate…"

"Supposedly killed," Spencer interjected.

There was silence on the other end of the call for several seconds.

"He's the Amir's son," Hall finally responded.

"Okay; even by our standards of inappropriate humor, that's not funny," said Danny.

"No, it's not," Hall replied, his voice flat and exhausted.

"I thought there was a screw-up in the lab results, so I had BND run it again. It's a ninety-three percent match for a child. Furthermore, we went to the hotel where we followed the man we saw leaving the murder scene at the warehouse. We entered the hotel room he was staying in and collected DNA evidence: hairs, fingerprints, etc. All belong to Abu Sul-Malik."

"What the actual hell!" said Spencer, more of an exclamation than a question. "Could it be another blood relative? With a strong DNA match?"

"That's what I thought as well," Hall replied, "But the fingerprints are an exact match to the Amir."

"But that guy looks nothing like him," said Abbasi and Danny in unison.

"No, no, no," Spencer began, his tone rising. "Hoooold up! Behnam, you said your guys could not find a trace of the Amir in the months you have been looking. Interpol, military, nothing… Is it possible he changed his appearance?"

"You mean plastic surgery?" questioned Abbasi.

"That's spy novel stuff, Spencer," Danny answered.

Abbasi turned in his seat to look at the other two men sitting in the back. The three of them exchanged glances in response to Danny's comment. A bit ironic, considering all three men had actually worked as spies in the past for the premier spy agency on the planet.

"Jesus Christ, that's it!" Spencer said, agitated. "That man is the Amir. Get that out to every agency—Interpol, CIA, FBND, the Pentagon, FBI, etc. The Amir has had plastic surgery to throw us off his trail. The son of a bitch has been walking around in plain sight for God knows how long."

Abbasi told his protégé, "We need to track down his whereabouts in Munich immediately!"

"We have a lead," said Hall. "A notepad in the son's room had the address and room number of a hotel in Munich. It's the Le Méridien, right next to the Central Train Station. It also had the word 'Babai,' which has a couple of different meanings. At first, we thought it referred to a woman, but when we ran the translation, we found that it also means Father in Albanian. It makes sense. We discreetly checked the hotel reservation records, and a 'Salim Hassan' is registered in room No. 612. Same name he was registered under at the Victoria Hotel in Nuremberg."

"Good detective work," Abbasi said. "Keep this up, and we might promote you to a desk clerk." Abbasi joked and hung up the phone. He liked the young agent Hall. He was a good kid, with superb instincts, even for an Ivy Leaguer.

"Seems like a great kid," said Spencer.

"He is," replied Abbasi from the front seat. "The 'new breed' coming in. Better skills, faster results, running all day and all night as long as they have a muffin and a latte," he laughed.

Spencer knew that if Abbasi didn't really like the kid, he wouldn't be giving him a hard time. Something you learn in the military. If you didn't like someone, you didn't bother. If you liked and trusted someone enough to have your back, you ragged on them like a younger brother. A lot of people didn't get the dichotomy in relationships among men in the services, which tended to carry over into their civilian lives once they left the military. But he understood it.

Abbasi had the driver pull over at the next Restplatz. The van followed suit. He gave the team an update on what they knew and the plan once they got to the hotel in Munich. This would be a story for the books, Abbasi thought to himself—one they could never tell or, at least, tell the truth about. But it would be a gratifying end to his agency career.

~~~

The Amir had kept his group of loyalists, Shahid-TB, quiet for the past two months to move some of them undetected into Munich.

Initially, he was going to bring them into Nuremberg, but his plans had not gone as hoped, and he had killed the former spy, John Spencer.

Now he would use his people and the group they had brought together in Munich—of the… how did the American politicians call it, 'disenfranchised' Muslims in this city?

Their numbers were not huge but were growing and enough to be effective. And besides, the more men you had, the more opportunities for leaks and failures.

Once the rest of his plan was executed, by blowing up the train station, the Muslim population in the city would begin to protest violently.

Abu Sul-Malik did not like failure. He would meet his son soon and make that clear to him. He had been making the boy dependent on his approval for years. His disappointment would surely enforce the boy's obedience, and if not…then the Amir did not have much use for him.

For now, he had things to prepare—backup plans and contingencies to ensure he avoided capture.

His men had scouted the hotel, looking for a means of escape should one be needed. There was an underground mall area below the main street level of this part of the city, which connected to the Bahnhof.
~~~

The hotel was a few blocks from the underground facility, but they had found access passages for electrical lines and plumbing that led to the main halls of the mall and close to the stairs of the station. He would walk this route with two of his men to learn the way, in case he needed to access it alone. He was nothing if not a meticulous planner, and he did not leave things to chance.

The Amir had checked into the hotel last night upon his arrival in Munich while his men sat in the van with their 'guest.'

Today, he went to his room, showered, and dressed in comfortable clothing—the style most Europeans wore, but too western for his taste. Abu needed to fit in and draw as little attention to himself as possible.

He wore dark blue jeans, a button-down white shirt, and a V-neck sweater with loafers. He felt comfortable and restricted all at the same time.

Abu made sure to leave his fingerprints on the doors and the desk, as well as all areas of the bathroom. He also made sure there was hair left on the brush. After all, if the CIA man known as Benham Abbasi did find him, he wanted to make sure the man felt gratification before meeting his end. It was ironic, really—finding your target just before they took you out. He smirked at the thought.

The Amir picked up a backpack he had carried from the country house and placed it on a small, round table. He unzipped the bag and pulled out one of the three devices that had been inside.

All devices were identical. A Semtex body and blasting cap, with the blasting cap detonator wired to an old model Nokia cell phone, blue and gray in color. These items were secured to small, cut wooden square boards.

The devices were safe, as the blasting caps were not inserted into the Semtex, and the cellular phone was not turned on. Thin layers of plastic wrapped around the blasting caps ensured no accidental insertion or charge took place while being transported. Small precautions, but minor details can mean the difference between life and death, as many of the pawns in his line of work had found out the hard way. The Amir did not want to risk being blown up by his own hand.

Each phone had a different number from a burner SIM card purchased under the table from a mobile phone repair business in the

Muslim community here in Munich. The clerk was one of the 'disenfranchised' of the community whose mosque had been closed two months ago. He was an immigrant from Syria, in his twenties, and angry—exactly the type of young men the Amir used around the world to carry out his work.

He put the device back where it had come from, zipped the bag, and placed it over one shoulder. Then he left the room.

The Amir and his men took the elevator downstairs to the main lobby and walked through the hotel to the staff hallway leading to the kitchen. They made their way to a door at the corner of the staff hallway, and one of his men pulled out two keys from his pocket. One he gave to the Amir, and the other he slid into the lock and turned until the door opened. The door was the entry to the passageway that led them underground and toward the mall and train station.

They walked through the door unnoticed by the kitchen staff, as the door was around a short corner from the main prep area. Once inside, they closed the door behind them. There were lights illuminating the concrete passageway. Metal braces were mounted along the walls, holding large to medium-sized cables in place. Some held electrical cables, while others held internet, phone, and TV cables. Pipes for cold and hot water and sewage that ran overhead were held in place by metal clevis hangers bolted into the concrete ceilings. The lights were run using conduits along the ceiling all the way down the length of the passageway.

The men walked approximately sixty feet, where the tunnel made a ninety-degree turn to the right and continued. They made the turn and walked another twenty feet, just a few steps before a metal staircase that led down to the next level.

The Amir instructed one of the two men carrying the backpack to place one of the explosive devices he carried behind a grouping of cables so it would be hidden unless someone was looking for it. The blasting cap was inserted into the putty of Semtex, and the Nokia cell phone was turned on.

The men walked about five more feet and turned to face the metal staircase that led to the level beneath the main structure of the hotel and under the city street. The terrorists descended the stairs, turned north, and made their way under Bayerstrasse facing the central train station.

The passageway went approximately one hundred feet and led to a set of stairs, which led upwards to a work hall at the main station and continued further, then turned to the west under the train tracks themselves.

The passageway split, leading in two directions: one to the left and one to the right. The passageway running to the left led up onto the main platform concourse area of the train station, situated between the train tracks and the food stands. The one to the right was smaller, narrower, and resembled a maze, filled with mechanical systems and heavy wire lines used for the electrical power of the train tracks. Abu Sul-Malik waited at the split while his men separated to place the remaining two devices.

The devices were positioned under different sections of the underground platform area to ensure that a larger section of track and transportation would be disrupted when detonated.

Once they finished placing the explosive devices, they backtracked to the stairwell that led to the central terminal. The men, including Abu Sul-Malik, walked out into the busy shopping area of the station platform, filled with small restaurant stands, coffee shops, and bakeries.

Abu Sul-Malik and one of his men walked toward the exit, where a black car was waiting in the parking lot for him. The other man walked toward the platform, where the train from Nuremberg was pulling in.

The Amir's henchman waited at the far side of the platform, with a full view of all the passengers exiting the train. He watched each person until he found the one he was waiting for.

~~~

Goran stepped off the train and walked to the edge of the platform, where he was met by one of his father's men. He was escorted through the shopping area, past the ticket machines and the hallway that led to the station office areas, to the station exit. He was brought to a black Mercedes-Benz, where the man opened the back door, and Goran climbed in to sit next to his father.

"Did you complete your task?" his father asked.

"He wasn't at home. He had packed his things and fled," the young man replied. "I had to kill the roommate."

"And where did the boy go?" his father asked.
~~~

"I don't know. I went back to the hotel, the Islamic center, even the mosque; there is no sign of him."

The car pulled out of the parking lot and headed toward the 'A8' south toward Feldkirchen.

"I have a surprise waiting for you."

Goran did not know where they were going. He had a feeling his father knew Avni had escaped. How he knew, Goran wasn't sure. But he knew his father did not want any loose ends to this operation. His identity was what kept him safe, and Babai would not risk anyone finding out. Even the majority of his loyal followers did not know who he really was. They knew he was the leader of the 'Shahid–TB' but believed he was a loyalist of Abu Sul-Malik, who had been killed almost a decade ago.

Goran wanted to take part in leading the group with his father, but some of his father's methods were far more gruesome than he could stomach.

Killing and blowing up buildings was something the younger terrorist could understand, but his father's extracurricular activities… that was something entirely different, and it scared him.

The boy would have to find it within himself to do whatever his father asked of him. The revenge his father sought depended on it. So did his father's approval. He had to prove his loyalty to his father again and again or die trying.

~~~

The man from the train station who had walked Goran to the car made his way back to the hotel, where he sat in the lobby. He ordered hot tea and read a German newspaper. He positioned himself with a clear view of the hotel lobby entrance.

The man in his forties had been with Abu Sul-Malik for many years. The Amir had given him the chance to serve under him, provided him with money to care for his family, and helped him provide food and shelter—something he had struggled to do for most of his life. The man's parents had been killed in a mortar strike in their small village when he was a teenager.

His benefactor had told him that it had been the infidels from America who had destroyed the village and ultimately killed his parents. This, however, was not true. It was one of the Amir's cells training in the
~~~

desert that had made the mistake and aimed the mortar rounds in the wrong direction. But the man did not, and never would, know the truth. As far as he was concerned, he owed Abu Sul-Malik his life and was willing to die as a soldier in the army of Allah, if need be, to repay the debt he owed.

He patiently waited to see if the man his boss had shown him a picture of would show up. If so, he was to call his leader immediately and await his instructions.

If the man did not come, his boss would be free to return to his room in the city and meet with the others who had been recruited. Although he knew what his boss really wanted by being in the city.

He had tried once before to repay the Amir by bringing him such a prize, hoping it would put him in good graces, but he was beaten and forced to take the woman away and kill her himself. The leader of 'Shahid - TB' picked his victims himself and for his own reasons. Occasionally, he would only abuse them sexually and let them go, even giving them money for their time and wounds—usually doing so just before leaving to avoid any police showing up and looking for him.

Now, he only had to sit, wait, and report.

Chapter 14

Spencer, Abbasi, and Danny checked into the Alpen Hotel München on Adolf-Koping Straße. It was a decent hotel, just three blocks from the Le Méridien and about two blocks from the Hauptbahnhof train station.

This would allow them to be close to the area, but with a few blocks of separation from which to run their operation in close proximity. The men checked in under the pretense they were old Army buddies back for a small reunion. That way, they didn't draw any additional curiosity, but in this part of the city, there were many visitors and foreigners, so it wouldn't make much difference. The three men checked in and made their way up the elevator to their rooms.

The rest of the team checked into the Maritim Hotel, half a block from the Le Méridien in one direction and just across the street from the Goethestraße side. This allowed the team to have a line of sight from one direction and the ability to be on site in less than a minute.

The team consisted of men who had never been part of Operation Grasshopper and were unknown to the Amir and his followers. They could move around the area undetected.

~~~

Agents Galloway and Carmine had been with the agency for twenty-three years. They had worked on operations all over the world, some together and some as part of other teams.
~~~

They were both consummate professionals with strong tradecraft. Blending into environments and situations was their specialty, and they were very serious about their work.

Galloway entered the Le Méridien hotel and made his way toward the back corner, where there was a small hallway and a coffee bar. He ordered an espresso and stood at a table at the edge of the short hallway, which gave him visibility of the lobby. He pretended to look at his phone but also took pictures of the people sitting in the lobby area. Only a few people lounged in the lobby.

A woman was on a mobile phone with a day planner she was agitatedly writing in. She would stop and raise her hands in a gesture to the person she was on the phone with, as if the caller could see her hand motions. Clearly, the woman was having a bad day. If the team didn't find something soon, her day could get a lot worse.

A younger couple sat with their luggage, going through papers from their backpack. It reminded him of the trip he and his wife had taken years ago across parts of Europe, checking their itinerary for trains as they checked out of each hotel.

Finally, there was a man sitting in a high-back chair facing the main entrance. The man had a newspaper up in front of his face, and the sides of the chair made it a little difficult to see his profile from where Galloway stood.

The doors to the hotel opened, and an older couple with a suitcase walked in and made their way to the check-in counter. Galloway noticed the man slightly drop the paper to see who had walked in. It wasn't much, but he had dropped the paper just enough for Galloway to get a picture of the man's face. He appeared to be of Middle Eastern descent and in his mid-to-late thirties.

Under normal circumstances, that wouldn't be enough to be suspicious. A man waiting to meet someone and of Middle Eastern descent was not enough reason to suspect someone.

But, given the situation, location, and apparent attempt to conceal his face, along with the fact that the man had not turned the newspaper page in the last ten minutes, this made it a pretty sure bet.

Galloway texted the man's picture and a quick sit-rep to Carmine, who was waiting around the corner.

Carmine called his boss to let him know they had a lead and detailed the man who was sitting in the hotel lobby, either waiting or watching. Whether he was waiting on the Amir or watching for Abbasi and the team was not yet known.

"Stay where you are and have Galloway continue to observe. I'll get back to you shortly," said Abbasi, and hung up the phone.

"Did they find something?" asked Danny.

"Hotel lobby of the Le Méridien. Appears to be a lookout. Galloway thinks he may be one of the Amir's men," replied Abbasi.

"What are the chances he leads us to the Amir?" Danny inquired.

"We could just wait it out, but it's possible he might make us wait and notify the Amir or someone else," Abbasi said.

"Then we lose the element of surprise," Danny said with disapproval in his voice.

"Or we could dangle a large carrot and see if he takes the bait," Spencer finally joined in. He had been listening and contemplating the risks and rewards of what he was about to propose. The risk was real, but the reward could be tracking down and finally taking out the Amir.

"Got a plan?" asked Danny.

Spencer looked up at Danny and glanced at Abbasi, who was regarding him with a questioning expression.

"As far as we know, the Amir has been targeting anyone associated with our team from Operation Grasshopper. At the moment, that leaves just you and me," Spencer said, looking at Abbasi.

"Correct. But since the bombing of the hotel room, they think you are dead," replied Abbasi.

"Exactly. So what if we force this guy to make a move, either toward us or to contact the Amir?"

"What do you have in mind?"

"What if we walk in together and the lookout sees us?"

"That would definitely get a response, but we are not completely sure he is one of the Amir's guys or that he isn't alone," Abbasi reminded him.

"Have the rest of the team set up at different points around the hotel. Scout it out first in case there is a sleeper somewhere. We can position guys at potential escape points and corner the guy when he makes a move," Spencer suggested.

"Could work," Danny interjected. "Exits, hallways, elevators, and we need at least one person close to the guy in case he goes for a weapon or a phone."

"At the moment, it seems like the only play we have," was Spencer's response.

Abbasi thought about this for a moment, considering the plan, the risk, the execution, and the number of guys he needed to pull it off. Was it worth it?

"We may need to bring the Federal Intelligence Service in for assistance, especially if there is potential for action in a public setting."

Abbasi called Carmine back and told him he needed to scout the hotel for potential exits, stairwells, etc., and calculate how many men would be needed and where. He needed it done quickly.

Abbasi then made a call to his contact at The Bundesnachrichtendienst and coordinated a dozen plainclothes men to meet him at his hotel to coordinate the operation.

~~~

The car pulled up to the country house. Abu and Goran got out of the vehicle and made their way inside.

Goran knew his father was upset about Avni getting away. Not much he could have done, as the kid had fled before Goran had reached the apartment. Plus, he had questioned the roommate, who didn't know anything, thus taking care of that loose end, as he knew his father would have wanted.

He followed his father toward a door that led downstairs to the basement area.

The walls were made of cement blocks, and the floors were concrete —dry and cold. The ceilings were low, just above seven feet tall, and the lights were single-bulb sockets with pull chains to turn them on. Old wooden shelves lined the walls of the farmhouse basement.

His father turned to him.

"Men make mistakes. They must learn from those mistakes and become stronger. If a man continues to make mistakes or fail…."
~~~

His father didn't finish the sentence, but he didn't need to. Goran knew the implied meaning. He understood that his father didn't accept failure from his men. Usually, he killed those who failed him or had them killed. His father was letting him know he had failed, and that was a strange feeling for Goran. He had never worried about his father's wrath toward him. He had always done as his father had asked and had attempted to do so this time. His father's words and the fact that he was brought to this basement gave him a sense of fear. For a moment, he considered that his father might kill him.

"I have always done as you have asked, Babai. Had the boy been at the apartment, or had I known where he had gone, I would have carried out your wishes."

Abu Sul-Malik stopped at the old wooden door at the end of the basement hallway and turned to his son.

"I am glad to hear this because you now have one chance to make up for the failure. And this time, you will do it my way."

The Amir opened the door, and Goran saw the scared young man, Avni, tied to a chair, cold and shivering. The smell of urine filled his nostrils.

A table sat to the side of the small room where one of his father's men had walked in and placed a rolled leather bag. His father took two steps over to the table, untied the straps around the leather, and unrolled the bag. Inside was a selection of different tools the Amir used for torturing his victims: an ice pick, a small bone saw, surgical vice grips, and forceps.

The son knew what his father expected. Under normal circumstances, he would never allow himself to take part in such atrocious acts. He would simply shoot the boy and walk away. But not this time. His father wanted obedience, assurance of loyalty, unquestioned compliance, and if he didn't comply, it may very well be him taking the boy's place.

"It shall be done, Babai," he said to his father.

The Amir walked out of the room, pulling the door closed behind him, smirking to himself as he turned toward the stairs. As he started to ascend the steps, he could hear the muffled screams of the boy behind him. He stopped for a moment, closing his eyes and relishing the moment. He remembered his first time, and it filled him with warmth. A sickening warmth.

Chapter 15

The BND sent fifteen agents to meet Abbasi: eleven men and four women. Most of these agents had counter-terrorism training, either from their military service or as previous specialized police officers who had been recruited to the BND for such work.

The plan was for some of these agents to walk into the hotel together as 'couples' and check in. Then they would make their way toward the elevator or hallways, coffee area, etc., without drawing additional attention from the target. They carried overnight bags and suitcases that concealed their Heckler and Koch MP5 machine guns while they carried their H&K VP9 concealed handguns on them.

Outside the hotel, other BND agents would cover the exits, just in case the man made it past the team inside.

Carmine and one of the other agents would move to the chairs just behind their target's chair and wait for any movement of a weapon or a phone.

Galloway had continued to check in with Abbasi and Carmine via text and had kept himself fairly inconspicuous. The target had turned the page of the newspaper once in two hours, only moving the paper when someone was entering or leaving the hotel.

One of the German agents had passed an earpiece to Galloway after entering the hotel.

All agents and team members were in place. It was Go Time!

Abbasi and Spencer had walked the few blocks to the hotel and staged outside and around the corner where Agent Carmine had been stationed for the past two hours. The two men walked into the hotel's main entrance.

~~~

The target looked up from his paper. Apparently stunned, he let the paper fall to his lap. Not only was it the man his employer wanted to find, but the other CIA agent, John Spencer, whom they had blown up in Nuremberg, was standing beside him. It was not possible; they had confirmation that the man, John Spencer, was dead from the blast. But he was standing at the entrance with the munafiq, the traitor, Behnam Abbasi.

Spencer and Abbasi began walking in the direction of the hallway that was just past the check-in counter, making their way toward the elevators.

The Amir's man watched them and turned in his seat to follow as they turned a corner out of his line of sight.

The man stood and started to follow them down the hallway to see which way they had gone. He was hyper-focused, so much so that he failed to notice the agents moving in around him. As he turned the corner from the hallway to the elevators, he saw the two men standing there, looking right at him. He reached for the gun that was in his waistband behind his back, but his hand never made it. Carmine placed the muzzle of his service weapon to the man's head while one of the BND agents placed the man in handcuffs.

Spencer walked up to the henchman and reached into his jacket pocket until he found a cell phone. No security code. It was a Motorola flip phone, most assuredly a burner. He opened it to the contacts and found only two numbers listed.

"Which one of these is for your boss?" The man puffed up his chest and looked straight ahead. "Ah, playing hard to get. I can appreciate that. I'm not so sure these nice people will like it that much, though," Spencer said, referring to the German BND agents.

"I'm quite sure he will become more cooperative in the near future," said Abbasi, more for the henchman's benefit than for his team's.
~~~

The agents took the man out the side door to keep the guests from becoming aware of what was happening.

Spencer, Danny, and Abbasi accompanied the agents to a safe house not far from the hotel to start interrogation proceedings and get what they could from the man they had in custody. All three hoped the man would cooperate. They didn't like where they knew things were headed if he didn't.

~~~

He didn't have much longer. He knew it was most likely a matter of minutes before he was dead. Avni had stopped screaming nearly an hour ago. Not because the pain had stopped, but because his voice had given out. He was dehydrated, and his screams had been so harsh that his throat had bled and finally gone silent.

Avni had, in fact, passed out from the pain a few times, but the man torturing him, the one he had known as Samir, had brought him back with smelling salts. Each time, his torturer had seemed reluctant to continue, but continue he did.

Goran had felt sick to his stomach when starting his task. But he understood deep down it was either the boy or him. Strangely enough, it didn't make him hate his father or despise him. In fact, he still wanted his father's approval and love, even though now he wasn't sure his father was capable of such emotions.

He started with the scalpel, slicing down the boy's leg, then using the ice pick under his nails and eventually pulling them out. The louder Avni screamed, the more approval he knew he would receive from his father. Goran tried to be creative, thinking about what his father would do, but was unwilling to go to such extremes. He even sliced off the boy's lips, not knowing what else to do. He felt lost in such endeavors but pushed through. He hoped the boy would pass out again and not revive. Goran wanted this to be over for both of them.

~~~

Abu Sul-Malik watched the video feed from upstairs on his laptop. It was apparent to him that his child did not know there was a camera in the room. It was difficult for the Amir to watch. Goran was so awkward with his tools. He had no experience, but he was happy that his son was making an effort and following through on his commitment. In time, he would get better. In time, he would become the real son the Amir wanted.

~~~

At an undisclosed site in Munich that had once been an old jazz bar, in the basement of a building in the industrial area of the city, the Germans had a safe house of sorts. Reinforced metal doors, soundproofing, and a location away from prying eyes. They had brought the man here to interrogate him and learn what they could about the Amir.

After an hour of 'creative' questioning, the man had given up a few details, saying he was to let the others know if Abbasi showed up. If not, his boss would return to the hotel for the night.

The man still refused to give up the details of their plans, however, and the team was trying to figure out a path forward.

BND was pinging the two numbers listed in the man's phone to see if they could locate the Amir. Until then, the trio was contemplating other ways to try and draw the Amir out.

Digital forensics were trying to recover any text messages that had been deleted from the phone. They needed to determine if there was an active threat in the city and if there were any predetermined procedures the group used to contact each other. Any covert methods employed to ensure they knew it wasn't someone else attempting to send a message.

They knew the Amir was smart enough to take precautions, which were needed to keep the terrorist from getting caught. If they could ascertain what those precautions were, they might have a way to reach out to the Amir or his men and attempt a strategy to take him out. Maybe they could lure the Amir back to the hotel and take him in his room. It was an option, but only if they could determine if there were special protocols in place first.

The agents were continuing to work on their prisoner when a new arrival walked in. A nondescript-looking man, carrying a box-shaped brown leather case, similar to what attorneys or doctors used. It looked old and worn; the man wore a loose-fitting, German-style suit, a trench-style raincoat, and horn-rimmed glasses.

The man walked at a normal and casual pace, but stiffly, with a dogged sense of purpose on his face. He looked somewhat meek in his appearance, but the feeling the three men got from him was anything but.
~~~

They knew what he was here to do. Services by such men had been used since the Middle Ages.

"I didn't think the Germans employed such tactics, but it looks like they are taking this threat as seriously as we are," said Abbasi. "Looks like our guest is in for a bad day."

It was implied and understood that the man who had just walked in and toward the back room where the prisoner was kept was an off-the-books interrogator. The kind that was not held to such policies and restraints as the Geneva Convention.

The rule of law said such "torture" techniques could not be used, and public opinion agreed. Many argued that information gathered under such duress was fallible, as someone being tortured would say anything to make it stop.

The verdict was still out for many who did this for a living or those who were tasked with saving lives and stopping terrorist attacks at any cost. Some details gathered had panned out in the past.

Was it morally wrong to use such tactics to save others? Was it immoral for these people to use terrorism to kill innocent people? The argument of 'two wrongs don't make a right' seemed simple and childish. The real world did not work in such simple sound bites. The prisoner always had a choice to come clean and provide answers and useful information when asked. If they cooperated, such tactics would never be needed or implemented.

Just then, one of the BND agents entered the main bar area where the three men were sitting.

"We could ping both phone numbers. Both are at the same location outside the city, in a rural area called Feldkirchen-Westerham."

"Can we dispatch a team to observe the location?" asked Spencer.

"We already have a team en route," was the reply.

"Please make sure they do not move in until we have confirmation that Abu-Sul-Malik or others associated with him are present," Abbasi instructed.

"Feldkirchen-Westerham is about thirty to forty minutes from here," said Danny. "We have a little time, but not much. Have Galloway and Carmine checked the Amir's hotel room yet?"

"Good question," Abbasi replied, then proceeded to pull out his phone and call Galloway.

Chapter 16

With the help of the BND agents on site, Galloway and Carmine were able to get the room number of Mr. Salim Hassan. After what happened at the Le Méridien in Nuremberg, the team was not taking any chances. They placed a 'Do Not Disturb' notice for hotel staff on the hotel room.

Once upstairs, the team used a few tools from the EOD technician the Germans had loaned to the agency.

A telescopic pole not much bigger than a dentist's mirror for your mouth, which had a video camera the size of a chocolate chip mounted on an oscillating joint at the end, was used to slide under the room door and send images to a screen showing any sign of a booby trap or explosives that could be set off by opening the door.

They looked for any beams of light that could be a light sensor trigger, light filament wire, or other such devices. Nothing was detected. The decision was made for the team to take the stairway down two flights until EOD opened the door and ensured the room was not a threat.

Minutes later, the team was back upstairs and in the room. They found exactly what the Amir had left for them. It was a bit of cat and mouse, and the Amir appeared to be enjoying himself.

The EOD tech walked up to Galloway and Carmine and gave them a status report. He had run a chemical sniffer around the room and found traces of Semtex on the table.

Carmine called his boss and let Abbasi know what they had found. The room had no explosive devices, but it did detect that Semtex had been present. Additionally, hair and fingerprints were all over the room, and he was sure they belonged to the Amir. The question was, where was the Semtex?

~~~

Spencer, Abbasi, and Danny arrived at a rally point about a quarter of a mile from the house that was under surveillance by the German counterterrorism team. This was a rural farm area called "Oberaufham."

With a population of less than one hundred thousand, the house was set back off the main road. This would be good if things went kinetic—less likelihood of civilian casualties.

Danny, who was fluent in German, went to get a sit-rep from the BND agents who had been watching the house.

The two remaining teammates stood quietly, watching Danny approach the BND agents and observing the general area for movement, egress, and choke points.

Abbasi turned to Spencer, observing the man for just a moment before asking,

"So, how are you dealing with all of this?"

"Which part?"

"I'm not too concerned about the operational aspects, John. I know you can handle that. How are you dealing with the other stuff? The reunion of sorts?"

Spencer took a moment to consider the question. There was a time when he would have brushed off the inquiry, puffed out his chest, or made some smart-ass reply to show his hard side—the warrior side, the side that nothing penetrated or bothered. But that man died a long time ago. To be honest, he had caused a lot of problems for himself and almost ruined friendships with the closest people he had ever had in his life. No, that was not who he was anymore, nor the person he ever wanted to be again.

"Honestly, Taco," Spencer used the senior man's nickname as a sign of friendship and personal connection rather than professionalism. "I feel grateful. I have a lot to make up for with Danny and Greta. I don't deserve them. But I plan to take advantage of the opportunity and repay it
~~~

in kind. A lot of whiskey under the bridge, Taco, a lot of whiskey under the bridge."

Abbasi knew at that moment that Spencer was ready. He had seen many of his former teammates and others while working clandestine operations with the agency who could never break out of the mindset of the 'badass bullet boy' mentality. They never grew past the instruments they were trained to be. Sadly, many faced some of the same issues that Spencer had: alcoholism, divorce, and estrangement from their kids.

But Spencer had found humility. He had faced his fears and owned up to his mistakes. Pretty enlightened for a knuckle-dragger, he laughed to himself. Yes, Spencer was going to be okay.

At that moment, Danny walked back up.

"Team says they have spotted three individuals. They appear to be guards. We assume the kid, Avni, and the Amir, plus one more, are in the house. Six in total."

"Normally, this would be a standard breach-and-execute, but we don't know what we don't know. For example, does the Amir have devices throughout the city with a remote detonator?" Spencer cautioned.

"And we don't know if there are others in the house that BND has not spotted yet," Abbasi stated.

"Suggest we continue to observe until we have a little more concrete detail on what we are dealing with," Danny

chimed in.

~~~

Goran was in the kitchen. He felt too sick to eat after what he had been forced to do to Avni. But his stomach was churning and growling to the point where it was giving him hunger pangs. He was trying to eat a sandwich to settle his stomach and drink a soda to settle his nerves. He had scrubbed his hands at the sink for what seemed like an eternity. The blood had dried and did not want to come off. It clung to him like a stain, a forever reminder of what he had done.

Killing was one thing. Slitting the throat of the roommate was easy —quick and done. But the long-term torture and the screams? He was not his father. This was too much for him.

At that moment, Goran's father entered the kitchen, followed by his guard.
~~~

“Ana fakhur bik ya abni,” I’m proud of you, Son. “A little squeamish for my taste, but you will learn to do better,” said Abu-Sul-Malik.

The thought of doing this again was not a pleasant one for his son.

“I wish I could stay and show you how to do it properly, but I have other things to attend to. Finish the boy and get to the airport. You will book a flight back to Pristina tonight. You will be texted a location to wait for further instructions.” And with that, Abu turned to leave. No goodbye, no hug, no sign of emotion from the psychopathic terrorist toward his son.

Goran was relieved that his father was leaving. He was also relieved he would not have to continue the torture. He wasn’t sure how the boy was still alive at this point, but it would bring him peace to end the boy's life.

~~~

It had been several hours since the team had arrived on site. Abbasi had called Agent Hall, who had made his way to Munich, to relieve Carmine and Galloway at the hotel so they could join him and the others at the farmhouse location and maintain a team of BND agents undercover in case the Amir returned. By this time, pictures of the Amir’s new identity had been sent to Abbasi’s team and those German agents assigned to him, as well as pictures of the other suspects in the Amir’s group. The pictures had been given to all concerned under the Amir’s alias. The true identity of the bloodthirsty terrorist was on a need-to-know basis, and most people did not need to know.

~~~

It was just past dusk, and the BND team watching the farmhouse spotted movement and taillights from one of the vehicles parked in the driveway. They notified the leader of the American team.

~~~

Galloway and Carmine had arrived on the scene and were standing with the rest of their team.

At that moment, Abbasi’s phone chimed. He answered it. “Just one? Got it,” and he hung up.

BND had just spotted one of the vehicles at the house starting up. “The three of us will tail the vehicle. Galloway, Carmine, stay here and coordinate with BND in case any other vehicles come or go. Keep me
~~~

posted." Abbasi wanted these two seasoned agents posted here. He knew their capabilities and professionalism. More than that, he trusted them.

The three senior members jumped in their car and waited with the headlights off. Not knowing which direction the car would go, they waited until it pulled out before they followed.

~~~

The Amir walked out the front door of the secluded farmhouse, feeling secure in his plan and knowing that no one knew he was alive or what he had planned. But they would know soon enough. They would all know he was very much alive, even if they weren't.

~~~

BND texted Abbasi that the passenger in the back of the vehicle matched the description of the businessman, Salim Hassan.

~~~

Abbasi looked at his phone, still trying to grasp the fact that this butcherous bastard was still alive. He closed his phone and matter-of-factly stated,

"It's the Amir. He is the passenger in the vehicle. One driver and one in the passenger seat. The Amir is in the back seat."

The other two sat silent for a moment, staring straight ahead like deer in headlights. Then they glanced at each other. These men were trained to stay calm, not to be anxious. Slow is smooth, smooth is fast—a saying that implied calm, methodical actions prevent mistakes. Even with all the years of training and combat action, knowing the Amir was only a car away from them sent a chill down their spines.

"Follow them. We have to know where they are going. Once we know where they are, we can take him down, but only after we are certain there aren't any other devices," Abbasi directed.

"And if we can't verify, we take him and torture the murderous bastard until he squawks," Spencer said flatly.
~~~

Chapter 17

The team followed the Amir's car all the way back to Munich.

As soon as they approached the city limits, Abbasi called Agent Hall to give him a quick summary and a heads-up that the Amir might be returning to the hotel.

~~~

Charlie Hall hung up his cell phone and placed it back in his jacket pocket. He took a deep breath in through his mouth and slowly out through his nose to calm his mind and a slight case of nerves. Investigating terrorists and bombings was something he could manage psychologically, but the potential of one of the world's most wanted terrorists, thought to be dead, planting explosives in hotels and God only knows where else—with the risk of civilian casualties—was more than he had dealt with before.

He had only been with the Agency for a few years. Most agents his age did not get these kinds of assignments or opportunities, mostly because they didn't have the skill or experience at that stage of their careers. But his boss, Case Officer Abbasi, had pulled him aside before his training at the farm was complete to interview him.

Charlie had been at the top of his class in both academic and tactical training and assumed that was why he was being interviewed for a slot somewhere at Langley. Little did he realize that Abbasi was about to give him the chance that would shape his career with the agency.
~~~

Agent Hall quickly notified the German team stationed at the hotel and ensured all access points were covered, including the room next to the one registered under Salim Hassan's name.

~~~

The Amir's driver circled back twice to ensure they weren't being followed. But Spencer, Danny, and Abbasi were not new to this game. It was simple spycraft, and they had practiced it for years. The vehicle finally pulled up in front of the Le Méridien hotel in Munich.

Abbasi was already on the phone with Agent Hall, providing a moment-by-moment update.

Danny, who was driving, pulled into a parking lot across the street from the hotel entrance. They watched as the second man, sitting in the passenger seat, got out and opened the back door for the main passenger to exit the vehicle.

The three seasoned warriors watched as the man, known as Salim Hassan, stepped out of the car. He paused for a moment to hand his bag to his security man, adjust his coat, and glance at his surroundings before walking into the hotel lobby.

The trio knew this was the man they were tracking—the one thought to be dead for years. They recognized him as Abu-Sul-Malik, the Amir.

The car's driver pulled away from the entrance and into the hotel's parking garage.

Abbasi relayed the information to Agent Hall, who already had members of the BND team stationed on different floors of the parking garage.

~~~

Goran had finished eating what he could of the sandwich. His stomach had been telling him he needed to eat, but after the conversation with his father, he could manage only a few bites. He left the kitchen and went up to one of the rooms in the house to take a shower. Maybe he would feel more refreshed and have a clearer head for the task ahead.

~~~

Galloway had just gotten off the phone with Abbasi. He filled Carmine in on the details about the Amir returning to the hotel. The two men made a plan to infiltrate the farmhouse and either take out or arrest the individuals inside.
~~~

They walked off to update the BND agents still watching the house.

They calculated that only three men were left in the house: one unknown terrorist, the killer presumed to be the Amir's son, and Avni Shala, the desk clerk from the hotel in Nuremberg.

~~~

The Amir walked into the hotel lobby, taking in his surroundings as he moved toward the elevators.

He noticed nothing unusual or out of place among the patrons in the lobby or at the check-in counter. He wondered if the Americans who had been hunting him had made their way to Munich after all. Surely, they would have shown their hand by now. The local police would be stationed around the hotel, with sirens blaring from every police car and bomb disposal units searching for his explosives.

But there was nothing. He hoped they would catch up soon. He would hate to execute his plan without the added bonus of taking out the last man responsible for hunting him down years ago. Satisfied, he walked past the coffee stand toward the elevator to the sixth floor, never noticing the American CIA agent sipping his coffee.

~~~

Parking the car on the third floor of the parking garage, the man from Syria opened the car door and strolled toward the stairwell. His mind was focused on the task ahead. Tomorrow, during the busy schedule for train commuters, there would be mass carnage and destruction—unlike anything these people had seen since their World War.

He relished the idea of killing these people. They were not followers of the Prophet, and they helped wage war against his country and the homes of his brothers. These infidels deserved to die, were his last thoughts as he walked past the large structural steel beam to his left. The beam was just large enough to conceal the hefty frame of the German BND agent and his Heckler & Koch P8A1 pistol with a suppressor.

~~~

As soon as Agent Hall had confirmation, he called Abbasi to let him know the driver had been taken down quietly.

"The Amir walked in, scanned the lobby, and headed to the elevators as if he had no worries in the world. A real psychopath, that one."

~~~

Abbasi relayed the news to the other two sitting in the car with him.

"What's the plan? Take him down in his room? Wait until he leaves the room? How do you want to play this?" was Danny's question.

"It looked like he was carrying a bag with him, and we don't know if he has another bomb in the bag or if he has other devices planted that he can activate at a moment's notice," said Spencer.

"We could have taken him out in the hotel lobby, but there were too many unknown variables. The Amir has a plan, and we need to stop whatever that plan is as much as we need to take him down. We can't stop the plan unless we know what it is," said Abbasi.

"So, what's the move?"

"Hall said the Amir seemed confident when he walked in, glanced around, but didn't seem to be concerned. I assume he doesn't think we are onto him or have caught up with the clues he left. We should be able to hide in plain sight in the lobby and wait."

Spencer thought about this for a second. His instincts wanted to rush in and take out the Amir. But he knew there was wisdom in Abbasi's approach. Just like the story of the bull and the son, 'let's walk down and screw them all.' "Agreed," said Spencer.

Chapter 18

Goran felt better after taking his shower. His muscles were tense and sore, as if he had been beaten up. His body was forcing itself to do something his mind didn't want to do. The stress and strain it placed on him felt like he had been in a fight. Nowhere near as bad as Avni was feeling at the moment, he thought. But it would all be over soon, and the boy would feel no more pain.

He made his way downstairs toward the basement door in the kitchen. His father's henchman was standing in the kitchen, smoking a cigarette, watching a football game on a television set above the refrigerator, and drinking a cup of coffee. Goran thought back to when he was a kid, playing football in the field with his friends. He wished for the days of his childhood now.

He opened the door to the basement and made his descent.

~~~

Carmine and Galloway, along with one of the BND agents, were ready to make their way into the farmhouse. They wore soft ballistic vests and had placed suppressors on all their weapons to minimize noise and deter prying eyes, including the media. The last thing either country wanted was a story of international terrorism and joint agency efforts condoned by a foreign government, which could cause immense issues for both nations. So, they worked as quietly as possible.
~~~

With their weapons drawn, they made their way around the back of the farmhouse while the other BND agents moved toward the front corners of the house to cover all sides.

As they approached the larger kitchen windows, they could hear the sounds of the TV—cheers and loud noises emanating from the screen, an odd contrast to the grim realities taking place inside the house.

Cautiously, they approached the window, peering through the corner of the glass to see one of the three men standing in the kitchen, looking up at a small television set with a cigarette in one hand and a coffee cup in the other.

Galloway looked at Carmine, who nodded his approval.

"As good a time as any," Galloway whispered and stood straight up in front of the window, weapon aimed high.

The movement caught the man's peripheral vision, and he turned to look out the window, but it was too late. Two quick taps through the glass, both to the chest, and the man dropped to the floor, along with the coffee cup, which shattered into a dozen pieces as it hit the tile below.

The BND agent with them radioed his counterparts to breach the front door. The three men at the back entered through the rear door.

The five men cleared the rest of the house quickly, verifying that no one else was inside.

"Where did the other two men go?" asked Carmine.

"There was a basement door in the kitchen," replied the German agent who had been with Galloway and Carmine. They quickly made their way back to the kitchen, where one of the agents was standing guard.

~~~

Goran was already in the basement, and since it had been soundproofed, he did not hear any of the commotion above him as the team cleared the rest of the home.

He had considered how to put Avni out of his misery, the boy he had pretended to be friends with. He had finally decided to use the gun, as it would be the quickest and most painless way to end the boy's life. He had already inflicted enough pain on him. The least he could do was to end his torment quickly and send him to his reward.
~~~

He stopped outside the door to the room where Avni was being held. The door and handle were stained with blood, already dried in part from when he had closed the door earlier. He knew the scene awaiting him once he opened the door would be far more gruesome and bloodied than anything he had ever carried out before. It would be seared into his brain for as long as he lived.

Goran opened the door with closed eyes. Upon opening them, he stepped into a room covered in blood—on the walls, on the floor, splattered on the ceiling, and it covered every inch of the boy lying on the floor. He stood there and paused, unable to take another step. The imagery gave him tunnel vision. His ears went deaf from the pulsing sound of his heartbeat, so much so that he never heard the men entering the basement.

~~~

The Germans entered the basement first, their H&K G95Ks at the ready. Entering in a clearing formation, the five men made their way into the basement. The German agents noticed a door at the far end of the hallway with a light emanating from within, casting a shadow against the wall.

The German team lead spoke in a commanding voice, "Verlassen Sie den Raum rückwärts mit erhobenen Händen." ('Step out of the room backwards with your hands raised.')

~~~

Goran couldn't bring himself to approach the body of the young man lying there. If he had, he would have realized the boy was already dead.

Goran could not stand the sight any longer. He raised his pistol and fired one shot into the boy's body before turning to rush out of the room, gun still in hand.

Exiting the room, all he saw was a bright flash of light.

~~~

Galloway made the call to Abbasi, who was now sitting in a corner of the hotel lobby, half-covered by a fake mimosa tree.

Galloway quickly gave his boss a situation report.

"The Germans are processing the scene quietly. No local authorities or media. So far, everything is being handled as expected. Unfortunately, we have not found any explosives or bomb-making materials in the farmhouse."
~~~

Abbasi instructed Galloway and Carmine to return to the hotel and wait outside for further orders.

Abbasi hung up and called Spencer, who was standing with Danny next to the elevators.

He gave them the rundown. Not finding explosives meant they had to be with the Amir. And that meant they had to continue to be very cautious in their approach.

Chapter 19

With his guard outside the door in the hallway, the Amir settled in for a few hours of sleep before preparing for the execution of his plan—and those unfortunate souls departing or arriving by train, of course. He smiled to himself.

They had tried to stop him. They hunted him and thought they had taken him out. But here he was, about to show the world he had survived, and he was out for vengeance. He only wished the remaining member of Operation Grasshopper was here so he could finish his business of eliminating all who had a part in it. He knew he would get his revenge eventually. The traitor Abbasi couldn't hide forever. The Amir turned off the light on the side of his bed and closed his eyes.

~~~

The German counterterrorism team had installed miniature, high-resolution cameras in the hallway of the sixth floor and in the room reserved under Salim Hassan's name, in anticipation of the Amir's potential return.

The team had cross-referenced the names of all guests checked into the hotel against both German and Interpol databases, as well as through the CIA for those of American and Canadian citizenship.

The passport photos of all registered guests were run through Langley and Interpol in case the Americans had any intel that the Europeans did not.
~~~

Surveillance video was being observed in real-time from the room next door to

the Amir's. It showed him entering the room, taking a shower, and going to bed. He did not check his cell phone, use an electronic tablet to access the internet, watch television, or engage in any other activities.

His guard had pulled a chair from the table in the room and placed it just outside the room in the hallway, to the right of the bedroom door. There he sat for several hours, never checking a cell phone, leaving to take a break, falling asleep, or showing any other weaknesses the team could exploit. To be fair, the guard was professional about his job. The surveillance was rather boring.

The surveillance crew stayed in contact with the rest of the team, who were located throughout the hotel, including Spencer, Abbasi, and Danny, who had been given earpieces by the German team so they could communicate with the rest of the teams on the ground.

Since English was considered the international language, most of the brief communications were conducted in English.

~~~

It was well past midnight when Abbasi walked over to the elevators for a face-to-face meeting with Spencer and Danny.

"What's your take so far?" he asked them.

Danny spoke first. "No sign he has the explosives on him, but I still don't trust that there isn't something larger at play here."

"Same," said Spencer. "Why this hotel? Same hotel chain as in Nuremberg. Coincidence? Doubtful. My gut is telling me there is another attack planned on the hotel, or he is using it as a base of operations, and the attack is imminent."

Abbasi nodded with a furrowed brow. He had been thinking about something very similar while sitting in his little hideout behind the plant.

"The Germans have scoured every inch of this hotel and found nothing."

"Have they walked the hotel with a sniffer?" Danny asked, referring to a mobile explosive detection device capable of detecting trace elements of various explosive residues in the air and on items. "If not, I brought one as part of my kit," Danny finished.
~~~

“Of course, you did,” Spencer said with a hint of playful sarcasm at his friend's expense. “You didn’t pack a sandwich by chance, did you?”

“I’ll tell Galloway to keep an eye on things while you grab the sniffer from your kit in the car. I don’t need you getting made or taken out in the parking lot. Greta would hunt me down. Make it quick.”

And with that, Abbasi radioed Galloway, ensuring the entire team was aware. Better to have multiple sets of eyes on the situation instead of just one.

~~~

Less than ten minutes after leaving his teammates by the elevator, Danny was now standing at the edge of the hotel’s kitchen doors in a small alcove with double swinging doors to the main kitchen and a locked access door to his right. He was hungry, but the feeling in his gut at the moment had nothing to do with needing to eat. He radioed his team.

~~~

“Guys, we have a problem. You should head toward the kitchen.”

Spencer knew Danny well enough, even after all these years, to detect the level of concern in his voice. He knew Danny had sensed something. He looked at Abbasi, and they both quickly left the elevator area and made their way to the hotel kitchen. They weren’t worried about missing the target. Surveillance was all over the two tangos upstairs and would alert everyone if there was any movement.

~~~

Abbasi

and Spencer walked into the little alcove area leading to the kitchen doors.

“I turned on the sniffer as soon as I entered the hotel to give it time to boot up. I wanted to run the sweep from the entry point through the hotel. As soon as it was up, I got a hit. It led here. The kitchen was closed, so I went through but did not pick up anything. But the door to the right is locked. Do we know what’s behind it?” Danny stood there, holding the sniffer in his hand.

Abbasi radioed the BND team on comms to ask if anyone had the blueprints for the building.

Three minutes later, an agent walked up to them with an electronic tablet displaying the hotel blueprints.
~~~

“Danny, walk the rest of the hotel to see if you pick up any additional traces while we go over the blueprints. We need to know all areas of potential risk,” Spencer said, knowing his friend didn’t need an explanation for the last part. Danny was all too aware of their risks and was placing himself in the middle of them to help Spencer.

Danny turned with the sniffer in hand and headed back to the main lobby.

Abbasi walked through the kitchen doors and placed the tablet on the stainless-steel prep table, bending over to swipe through pages of drawings, looking for the door and where it led. Spencer joined him.

~~~

It was nearly 4:00 AM, and the lobby was completely empty except for the single night clerk, who was busy handling paperwork from the busy day shift.

Danny walked around the perimeter of the lobby, losing any detection of explosives until he returned to the coffee shop and the entryway to the elevators.

Danny walked in and around the coffee shop, detecting no traces of explosives, although he saw a croissant in the display case. He hadn’t eaten in what felt like two days.

He slid the cabinet door to the right, grabbed the croissant, and took a large bite while sliding the cabinet door shut and making his way to the elevators. The sniffer detected trace elements again.

“Up we go,” he said to himself as he pressed the button for the elevator.

Stepping into the elevator, Danny was mindful of the guard on the sixth floor, so he pressed 2-5 and 7-9, leaving the sixth floor alone. His plan was to step out of the elevator for a moment to see if the sniffer detected anything, then back into the elevator before it closed.

“Let’s hope this works.”
~~~

Chapter 20

Danny walked back into the kitchen, where his two colleagues were mid-conversation.

Both men stopped and looked at Danny for details.

"Trace elements were detected all the way to the elevator. I've checked all floors except for the sixth, for obvious reasons, and found no detection on any of the other floors."

"The sixth floor was checked, especially Amir's room, and no explosives were found," Spencer replied.

"They said they detected Semtex with a sniffer but didn't find anything. It's possible they were brought to the hotel room and then taken elsewhere," Danny offered.

Abbasi interjected, "The door leads to an underground utilities tunnel for electrical, water, sewage, and internet. It also connects to a tunnel that runs under the Central Bohnhoff Train Station. Depending on the amount of explosives, it could take down the entire hotel, causing mass casualties."

Just then, the BND agent walked up with a key.

"We had the Germans get the key to the door so we could investigate," said Spencer.

Danny pulled out a cable line and what looked like a cell phone from the small black bag he had brought in from the car.

"We're not opening anything until we know it's not rigged," Danny said, looking at all three men standing in front of him. He connected the cable to the device and powered it on.

The cable had a miniature camera attached to the end of it, and the cell phone acted as a small monitor. Danny slid the cable under the door in the alcove and twisted it inch by inch to survey the area around the door. "Ready."

The German agent used the key for the door, but it wouldn't go all the way into the lock. He tried several times, to no avail. The agent ran back to the front desk and sternly reprimanded the clerk for giving him the wrong key. The clerk assured the agent that he had given him the only key they had to the door.

"I wondered if I would ever get to use these," quipped Abbasi as he pulled out a small pouch containing a lock-picking tool set, compact enough to fit inside a jacket pocket. He began one of several attempts to unlock the door.

After a few minutes and more than a couple of attempts, he had it. "Got it" were his only words.

He stood and looked at both men standing in front of him. They both gave their non-verbal approval. But before Abbasi turned the doorknob, the surveillance team came over the comms. "Subject one is up. Repeat, subject one is up."

"You two head back to the elevator. I got this," Spencer told them.

"You sure?" asked Danny. "You don't know who else might be down there."

Spencer gave a slight smile. He felt his friend's concern. "Easy day," he said.

Spencer looked to Abbasi, and the two men locked eyes for a brief moment, exchanging acknowledgment of the seriousness the next few minutes might hold. Spencer gave Abbasi a slight nod, fully committed despite his earlier reluctance to be involved.

Spencer drew his pistol, which had an attached flashlight under the muzzle, opened the door, looked inside, and walked through the opening, letting the door close behind him.

Abbasi walked off around the corner, making his way back to the elevators. Danny hesitated for just a moment, looking at the closed door, hoping it would not be the last time he saw his friend. Then he turned to catch up with Abbasi at the elevators.

Spencer slowly walked through the cramped space of cables and pipes that ran along the ceiling and walls of the cement-enclosed tunnel. Dozens of wrapped cables and wires in various colors were connected by numerous metal connectors, some attached and some unattached to the walls and main metal frames holding them all in place. There were countless places to hide a small bomb or explosive device, making it feel like finding a needle in a haystack.

Spencer paused before continuing into the tunnel. He needed a plan to find the bomb.

"Work the problem," he told himself. "What could help me locate the device or devices?"

Spencer tackled the problem the way he had been trained to.

What details did he have that could assist him? What was he looking for? An explosive device, presumably crude and unsophisticated.

What was this based on? The fact that the other device in Nuremberg had been basic Semtex and a blasting cap, triggered by an older model cell phone. An extremely simple device, like IEDs (Improvised Explosive Devices) and VBIEDs (Vehicle-Borne Improvised Explosive Devices) that had been used throughout Iraq and Afghanistan.

Spencer continued along this train of thought.

What features of the device made it stand out or visible? He considered each piece individually. Semtex is just a block of putty. Since 1991, different types of Semtex had been given signature odors and colors to help identify and detect them for EOD and law enforcement. Unfortunately, the type of explosive used in Nuremberg was pre-1991 and had no color or odor, so that was not helpful.

Cell phone, he thought. What features could help him locate a cell phone quickly?

I don't have the number, so I can't track it that way. It was an older model phone, so it wouldn't have the embedded GPS application to locate it, and I don't have the equipment, even if it did.

He started at the beginning. Cell phone. Turn it on, and the phone boots up. Then what?

That's it, he thought. It boots up; it lights up. The phone screen would have to be on — faint glow or not, if it produces light, he should be able to see it in the dark. The tunnel had lights along the ceiling. Spencer thought there had to be a switch for the lights somewhere close to the entrance.

Spencer turned around and looked at the door he had just entered through. He searched the doorframe and the walls next to the door. Embedded in the cement wall was a square metal box. The door to the box was locked, of course.

Spencer pulled the chain around his neck out from under his shirt, connected to a Kevlar sheath. This was the knife he had taken from Danny's bunker. He drew the blade, made from reinforced high-carbon steel, and used it to pry open the panel's door. There, Spencer found the switches that turned off the lights to the tunnel and the backup lighting system. He knew it would take a few minutes for his eyes to adjust, but afterward, he should be able to detect even the slightest light source. He lifted his hand to the switches, and in one motion, everything went dark.

Chapter 21

Agent Hall had been standing and patrolling the parking garage for hours, along with two other BND agents. It was not the glamorous fieldwork he had been expecting since Nuremberg.

His adrenaline had been high since the hotel bombing and had remained elevated through the investigative work he had been doing with the German Federal Intelligence Service. Not to mention the shock of learning that the Amir was alive and had a son.

His cell phone buzzed. It was his boss, Benham Abbasi. Charley considered himself lucky. He didn't know what to expect when he was chosen to work for Abbasi on the Counterintelligence Team. Abbasi was Iranian. Charley hadn't been aware of Abbasi's background at the time and was curious how an Iranian came to work for the CIA hunting down terrorists. But he quickly learned who his boss was and what he was made of, and he was grateful to be mentored by the man.

Agent Hall answered the call.

"Hey, Boss."

"Head downstairs and meet up with Carmine. The two of you and two of the Germans are going to the central station. We think the bomb is in a tunnel under the hotel, and that tunnel connects to another one that goes under the station.

Spencer is in the tunnel now, looking for the bomb. The surveillance team is still monitoring the Amir and his guard. I want you guys at the central station just in case anyone is there or something happens. Also, if Spencer gets all the way through the tunnel, he may need backup."

"On my way," he confirmed to his mentor and hung up the phone, quickly making his way down the garage stairs to the ground level, where Carmine and two other BND agents were waiting.

~~~

Spencer sat on the metal grate step leading from the doorway of the hotel to the floor of the tunnel, waiting for his eyes to acclimate to the darkness.

It had been about ten minutes of sitting in total darkness.

Spencer knew it took twenty to thirty-five minutes for the rods in the eyes to adapt to darkness and, on average, about forty-five minutes to mostly acclimate. He hoped the ten minutes allowing the eye's cone cells to regain retinal sensitivity would be sufficient for his purposes.

He knew he had little time. But he also knew that taking things in a slow, methodical manner would eventually be the quickest way to find the device or devices.

Spencer grabbed the handrail next to him and stood up. The only thing he had to worry about was the brackets on the wall next to him holding the wires and cables. There were no drop-offs or edges where he could twist an ankle that he had seen prior to turning off the lights.

He slowly made his way down the tunnel hall, hands in front and to the side of him, feeling both sides of the wall as he walked. He scanned the ceiling and walls for any sign of a light source.

Spencer judged the distance of the tunnel as being approximately fifty feet from the doorway. He counted each step as an approximate foot in length while maintaining his balance with his hands against either side of the wall and continued to scan for light. Walking in the dark wasn't like walking in the light. It was like being blind and not knowing where you were going. It wasn't a quick process.

Coming up on what Spencer calculated was approximately sixty feet, he felt a dead space to his right, suggesting the wall on his right ended. He reached out in front of him a few more inches until he felt the wall in front of him. "So, we go right." Spencer adjusted his position to follow the tunnel to the right and re-centered himself, with arms stretched and balanced against the walls to his left and right.
~~~

He followed the wall for approximately ten feet until he could make out a faint glow coming from further ahead. His heart started to beat faster. 'Take a breath. In through the mouth, out through the nose,' he reminded himself. A breathing exercise used to calm his breathing and heart rate. He needed to be calm and in full control.

Making his way forward faster than before, Spencer stopped, looking at the dim glow coming from behind a grouping of internet Cat5 cables. He drew his pistol to use the flashlight attached. Holding the gun and light in one hand, he used his other to slowly and carefully part the cables until he could see the device.

A block of Semtex, a blasting cap, and a cell phone attached to a small piece of wood as a base. The cell phone was connected to a wire that was soldered to the blasting cap. Spencer had to use both hands to remove the device and opted for his cell phone's flashlight instead of his weapon. Replacing his pistol and pulling out his cell phone, he turned on the phone's flashlight and placed the phone in his shirt pocket to see what he was doing and to use both hands to try to disarm the device. He took a few long moments to examine the entire setup to ensure he hadn't missed something that could inadvertently blow him up in the process.

Satisfied with what he saw, he gently removed the blasting cap from the Semtex and used his knife to cut the wire from the blasting cap to the phone. He had to risk removing the entire setup from behind the grouping of cables and hoped there wasn't a hidden secondary trigger behind the wood base that would activate the Semtex once moved.

Spencer placed both hands on the edges of the wood board, using his thumbs and index fingers to gently grab hold.

"brrrrr brrrr," buzzed Spencer's cell phone in his shirt pocket.

He wasn't sure if he jumped higher or if his heart did. In all the firefights and situations he had faced over his career, he couldn't remember one that scared him as badly as his cell phone had at that moment.

"Your timing sucks," he said, answering the call.

"Any luck?" Danny asked on the other end.

"I found Joy. She's dead. Same setup as the last one," Spencer replied, referring to the bomb used in Nuremberg.

"You think there are any more?"

"I don't know. This tunnel connects to the Bohnhoff. It depends on what the Amir's plan is."

"You need to hurry; he is out of bed and getting ready. Agents Hall and Carmine are at the station with a couple of BND guys, just in case."

"I will keep looking. There is a lot of ground to cover down here, and I just blew my night vision."

"Wait, you grabbed the NVGs?"

"No, I... never mind, I'll explain later. Give me a heads-up if they head my way." Spencer hung up the phone. He looked back at the wooden board with the bomb components attached and decided there was no time to be timid. He grabbed the board and pulled it out. Not having blown up, he cut the zip ties holding each of the items to the board and then looked for a place to hide it.

Spencer could see that the tunnel extended past the staircase and made another turn. He walked the length of the tunnel another thirty feet until it turned again. Around the corner, everything looked the same as it did behind him, except for a couple of bags on the floor.

One of the bags was a European-style canvas clamshell satchel with handles. It appeared someone had been down here doing repair work on the lines and had left their tools and equipment behind, no doubt planning to return. There were two additional plastic bags containing small spools of wire and electrical tape that appeared to have been purchased from a local hardware store.

Spencer emptied one of the bags and placed the Semtex and board inside. He looked for a place to hide it. Glancing up at the ceiling, he realized the larger water pipes were close enough together that he could hide the bag on top, and it would not be visible unless someone looked above the pipes to find it. He made a mental note to come back for it.

Spencer turned and quickly backtracked his way to the staircase leading down.

"I hope you know what you're doing, Spence," he said to himself as he started down the steps.

~~~

Agent Hall and Carmine were walking through the central train station, watching as the early commuters stopped for their coffee and breakfast before getting on the train and heading to work.
~~~

The BND agents were positioned one at the entrance and one at the exit to the main hub. Once things got busy, Agent Hall thought they would need more hands on deck.

~~~

Surveillance radioed the team that the Amir was walking out of the room.

Both American and German agents were scattered throughout the hotel in anticipation.

Abbasi wondered if he should have made the call to evacuate the hotel. But he knew the movement would have shown their presence and alerted the media, and the Amir might have escaped or set off another bomb before Abbasi and the team had a chance to find it.

This was a risk, but one he and the Germans agreed to.

Danny decided to stay close to the elevator and convinced Abbasi to return to his original spot since the Amir most likely knew what Abbasi looked like, but not Danny, since Danny had not been a part of Operation Grasshopper.
~~~

Chapter 22

The Amir stepped out from the bedroom door and looked at his guard, then glanced up and down the hallway.

"Where is Ali?"

"He must be in the lobby; he did not come up last night," the guard responded in Arabic.

"Ali did not come up after parking the car? Did you speak with him?"

"No, Amiri," he replied, bowing his head and using the Arabic word for 'My Prince' in reference to his leader.

"I will deal with you later for such incompetence," said the Amir as he made his way to the elevator, followed by his guard. Abu-Sul-Malik assumed either the CIA or the German Intelligence Services had taken his driver, which meant they knew he was here. But did they know what he looked like? How much did they know?

"Give me the key," he demanded of his guard, who pulled the key from his pocket and handed it to his leader. The Amir assumed the authorities knew who he was now, but if they didn't, he might escape and finish his work. He wasn't so sure about this man. He wasn't that smart, and he was better used as a distraction.

"Take the elevator to the main floor, walk to the station, and wait by the entrance. I will meet you there."

"Amiri?" the man asked, confused.

"I'm taking the stairs. Because you did not notify me that Ali did not return last night, we cannot be sure that those who seek to destroy our cause did not take him. We must ensure nothing gets in the way of our plan. I will take the tunnel to the train station and make sure the devices are still in place. I will meet you there."

The Amir knew the chances of this loyal idiot making it out of the hotel would be very slim. His only hope was that it would provide enough distraction for him to make it to the tunnel and ultimately escape apprehension.

The Amir turned to walk to the stairwell as his henchman pressed the down button on the elevator.

~~~

Spencer was making his way through the tunnel by the light from his cell phone. Checking behind all the wires and cables and on top of the pipes was taking longer than he was comfortable with. Once he reached the bottom of the staircase, the tunnel went north and south.

Spencer pulled out his cell phone and opened the map application, typing in directions to the Munich Central Bahnhof.

He was approaching a set of stairs that had a lot more light shining through a door. According to his map, he was at the edge of the station. He assumed that was where the light was coming from.

He climbed the steps and peered through the window of the door at the top. It was a lit corridor that looked like an employee access hall, with doors on one side. Spencer tried the door. It was unlocked.

Spencer was worried that there were more devices planted here. He had to find them before the Amir had a chance to kill or harm anyone else.

~~~

Abbasi was on edge. The surveillance crew had radioed that the guard had passed something to the Amir and that he had taken the stairwell while the guard was on the elevator.

Divide and conquer? he thought.

"Don't let the guard make it out of the hotel," he radioed to the team.

Then, he called Spencer's phone to give him an update.

~~~

Spencer's phone began to vibrate, 'brrr, brrrr.'
~~~

He didn't jump quite as high as last time. Must be something about not being in the middle of defusing a bomb that helps calm the nerves, he thought.

"I'm still looking," he answered.

"The Amir is heading down now. The guard is in the elevator. The Amir is in the stairwell. I think he is using his guard as a distraction so he can slip past us."

"Let him," Spencer said. "If he heads to the tunnel, let him. There are only two more exits from the tunnel other than the station."

"I have those covered," Abbasi assured him. "And I have Hall and Carmine with two Germans at the Bohnhoff."

"I'm at the workers' entrance just outside the utilities tunnel. I have diffused one bomb but haven't found the others. I'm assuming if there are more, they are here at the station. Get on the horn and stop all incoming and outgoing trains and get more agents here now. Evacuate the station as fast as you can. If he comes this way, we have him trapped."

Spencer hung up and continued his search. He wasn't much for religion, but he took a moment to ask the Lord for a little divine intervention in finding the remaining bombs as he continued down the hallway.

~~~

The Amir was at the bottom of the stairwell, looking out the window to the hallway for any movement or activity. He wanted to see if his guard would be apprehended before he took his chance to make his way to the tunnel entrance.

The elevator dinged, announcing its arrival on the ground floor. Its door opened, and the man from Syria, who had been a loyal follower of the Amir, looked out into the hallway with trepidation. He cautiously stuck his head out of the elevator. Not seeing anyone, he stepped out and slowly made his way down the hallway connected to the main lobby, next to the small café area. He was sweating. His steps were half the stride they normally were, and his breathing had become shallow and rapid. He was scared. He looked around the lobby, from the corners to the chairs and sofas, the front desk, and each person in the area.

No one seemed to pay him much attention. Was he scared for nothing? He walked past the café and the front desk, heading toward the
~~~

hotel doors. He was going to make it. Only thirty feet left to go, twenty-five, twenty.

“Unten auf dem Boden,” "Down on the Ground,” one of the German Bundesnachrichtendienst agents yelled, pointing his firearm at the man.

Suddenly, multiple agents surrounded him, all with weapons drawn, yelling for him to get down on the floor.

Hearing the commotion, the Amir took a breath and calmly stepped out of the stairwell doorway along the left wall just to the left of the elevator and walked around the corner toward the lobby with his eyes straight ahead and his hand gripping the key to the door of the tunnel entrance.

Danny was standing around the corner from the elevator. He couldn’t be seen unless someone stepped to the right of the elevator. This vantage point gave him a clear sight of anyone coming off the elevator or walking down the hallway.

Danny had been monitoring the comms when he heard that the Amir was taking the stairs. He waited until he heard the stairwell door open and followed about twenty steps behind his target, with his weapon drawn. It would have been easy to put a bullet in this monster’s head at that moment. But Abbasi and Spencer wanted to play this out and make sure they didn’t miss anything. They wanted to keep more people from dying. Danny was on board with that.

Abbasi had already given the word to let the Amir go through the tunnel. If he tried to exit the hotel, take him down, but if he was headed to the tunnel door, let him go undetected.

The Amir made a turn just past the front desk toward the kitchen.

‘Ok, so tunnel it is,’ Danny thought to himself. He observed the Amir head into the little alcove area and place the key in the lock to open the door. He hesitated for a moment. Fumbling in his jacket pocket, he pulled out a cell phone and turned on the flashlight. He stepped through the door and let it close behind him.

Danny grabbed his phone and called Spencer. “Rat is in the trap. Watch your six,” and hung up. He knew Spencer had too much on his plate to waste time talking.

Danny motioned for one of the German agents to relieve him and then walked over to Abbasi, who was standing at the edge of his little hideout area off the lobby, watching as the lead BND Commander redirected most of his team to the train station to assist with a quick evacuation.

Abbasi had already called Hall, who was working with station personnel and the BND, to conduct an immediate evacuation of employees and civilians and to stop all trains from leaving or arriving at the station until this was finished.

"He's in the tunnel. I have one of the agents guarding the door to make sure he doesn't come back through," Danny offered.

"How's our boy?"

"Busy, would be my guess."

The two men made their way out of the Le Meridien and walked toward the Bohnhoff.

Chapter 23

Spencer had made his way through the hallway quickly. There were no cables or hiding places unless the explosives had been hidden behind one of the doors leading to the food and coffee stands on the other side. Spencer doubted that was the case. Too much foot traffic and too many chances of being discovered.

He continued until the hallway narrowed and, according to his phone's GPS, went under the train tracks themselves. There were several sections of tracks, and Spencer was concerned it might be more than he could search in time. "The only easy day…" he thought to himself and moved forward with his search.

The Amir was angry. He had now lost the two men he was counting on to get him out of the city once he detonated the last of the bombs.

One was most likely captured or killed last night, and now the idiot who failed to inform him of his missing associate had to be given up to the authorities so he could escape.

Now, the lights in the tunnel had been turned off, and he did not know how to turn them back on. What else could go wrong? he thought.

The Amir paused momentarily to consider his son. He wondered if the house had been discovered and if his son had finished his assigned task. He was less concerned about his son's fate and more about whether he had dealt with the boy. If Goran had been captured or killed, that was the price to pay. Abu-Sul-Malik then focused back on the matter at hand and did not think of his son again.

He made his way as quickly as he could, hoping no one would follow him into the tunnel, but he wasn't moving as swiftly as he would have liked.

Spencer was now under one of the sections of track. It was a mechanical maze full of wires and metal levers, gears, and other parts, all woven together into the components that make the train system work. He was carefully climbing over sections of equipment and deciding where to place his hands or feet. He wanted to make it out of this alive, and with all of his fingers and toes, if possible.

He could hear the high-pitched squeal of the train brakes coming from the section of underground train tunnels he had not yet reached. He seriously did not know if he could find the device in time and considered calling Abbasi to take the Amir out before he had the chance to blow it up. It would give them time to search every inch of the place to find the explosives. But if it wasn't here, where was it? It was a calculated risk to keep the Amir alive, following him in an attempt to discover what he was up to and to try and save lives. He hoped it would work. Time to check the next section.

Climbing back over a section of electrical cables, his eye caught something sticking out from the edge of a structural metal beam. He squinted to focus his sight. Was that…wood?

Agent Hall had considered the situation they were currently in: looking for a bomb in a train station full of tracks and mechanical areas. They were searching above ground, below ground, and right now, John Spencer was the only person actively looking.

Danny Doyle had radioed the team earlier upon Spencer's confirmation that the bomb in the tunnel was the same as the one in Nuremberg, which meant it used a cell phone as the trigger.

Agent Hall asked one of the German agents with the team if they carried a cell phone jammer with them. The agent said they carried the equipment in their vans but had not activated it since the Americans were continuing to use cell phones to communicate with each other.

Agent Hall barked an order to the man, over whom he had no operational control, to activate the jammer immediately.

"The devices are triggered by a cell phone. If the signal gets through, it blows up! Activate it now!"

The German intelligence officer radioed his team immediately over the comms in German rather than English, relying on his instincts because of the urgency of the issue. His voice and words were fast and urgent, and his tone was commanding.

The Amir had reached the section of the tunnel by the staircase where they had placed the first device. He wanted to check that it was still ready to blow once he called the cell phone to trigger the device.

His plan was to set off the bomb once he was at the station, causing a diversion at the hotel and drawing attention and resources away from the train terminal, allowing him to escape and blow the station all at the same time. Chaos would ensure his way out. He searched behind all the wires for several feet but could not find the device.

"Kol Khara!" he said out loud, which was an Arabic curse word—his way of expressing that his plans had all turned to shit. He hoped they had not discovered the others at the train station.

Abu Sul-Malik had no choice. He could not turn back. He had to continue to the station and hope he could still make his escape. The Amir pulled a gun from his waistband, hidden behind his back by his jacket. With a gun in one hand and his cell phone in the other for light, he descended the steps and continued making his way toward the Bahnhof.

~~~

Spencer deactivated the device. It was identical to the one he had disarmed earlier in the tunnel.

He tried to call Danny to let him know, but there was no signal. 'It must be all the metal down here,' he thought.

Hoping it was the last device, Spencer walked out from the section under the tracks and back into the employee entrance hallway, making his way forward to the steps that led up and out onto the main platform.

~~~

Abbasi and Danny had just arrived at the station and met up with Agents Hall, Carmine, and Galloway.

Hall updated them on his decision to activate the signal jammers for the cell phones.

"Holy shit, that's a hell of a rookie mistake on my part," Abbasi admitted. "It's a miracle none of those devices have gone off yet. Quick thinking on your part, Charley. You just might make it as an agent one day," the senior agent said to his protégé.

He sincerely liked the kid and thought he would be one hell of an asset for the agency. If he didn't like the kid, he wouldn't give him a hard time. He could see it in Agent Hall's face; he understood that.

At that moment, they saw Spencer walking out of the doorway leading to the main platform.

~~~

Abu Sul-Malik was at the steps leading to the station's employee hallway. He took a few steps up and looked out the window of the door leading to the hallway.

He did not see any movement. It appeared that the coast was clear.

~~~

Spencer looked around the station; it was mostly deserted except for the German agents he could see spread around the perimeter of the station walls and platforms. Good, he thought, they could evacuate the station. He noticed Abbasi and Danny walking his way from the other side of the food court, close to the entrance.

He began to make his way toward them, but something stopped him. Where was the Amir? It had been a while since Danny had called him to say the Amir had entered the tunnel.

Instinctively, Spencer drew his handgun and turned back toward the doorway he had just walked through.

Appearing from out of the door and into plain view was the Amir. His cell phone was in one hand, and a gun in the other.

The Amir looked at the man standing in front of him. It took a moment for him to rationalize it all. Then it finally hit him. The infidel spy, John Spencer, was not dead. He had not been killed in the blast in Nuremberg. Questions rushed through his mind. How was he here at this moment? Had he figured out the Amir's identity? Had he followed him to Munich?

He looked past Spencer to see the traitor Benham Abbasi standing behind the infidel.

Abu Sul-Malik, the Amir, realized he would not escape. He took some solace in knowing he would die taking out both men at the same time.

His only option was to blow the station up with himself and the infidel who had tracked him and was now pointing a gun at him.

He did not say a prayer to Allah. It was a futile effort, in his opinion. He did not believe in seventy-seven virgins awaiting him.

Abu Sul-Malik had already pulled up the number of one of the devices and pressed the call button on his phone, closing his eyes.

Spencer stood there, staring at the man who had killed his former teammates, who had caused so much death and carnage for so long. He was unemotional.

He waited, watching the Amir's actions.

The Amir lifted the cell phone back up to his face in a panic and pressed the call button again and again, but nothing happened.

He looked up at the man in front of him, the man he had followed to this country. The last man he had wanted to kill for tracking him down and forcing him into hiding for so long. He was enraged that his plans had been stopped.

He felt like a trapped animal, ready to lash out.

The Amir screamed and lifted his gun simultaneously to kill the man in front of him, firing blindly as he lifted the weapon.

~~~

Spencer waited for the moment. He was calm, his breathing steady, his heart rate normal.

John Spencer saw the evil standing in front of him. He saw the anxiety on his face, then the rage. Spencer watched as the terrorist, filled with rage, lifted his gun and started firing.

Spencer's face showed a slight half-grin as he gently squeezed the trigger of his FN 545.

The bullet hit its mark before the Amir could hit Spencer. The bullet penetrated the Amir's forehead, dead center, exiting and hitting the door behind him.

The Amir stood motionless for nearly two seconds before dropping to the floor.

It was over. No more second-guessing. The terrorist formerly known as the Amir was now dead. For certain, this time.

The German BND members and the other CIA agents rushed to the spot where the very dead man lay and began processing the scene.
~~~

~~~

Danny walked up.

"You okay?" he asked his friend.

"Yeah, I'm good. Better than he is," Spencer jokingly said, motioning toward the body of the dead terrorist with his head. Spencer turned to look at Abbasi, but he wasn't there.

Spencer turned back to where the two men had been standing and saw Abbasi standing there with his hand inside his trench coat. He looked up at Spencer with an expression that was a mix of confusion and, "oh shit."

Spencer and Danny ran up to the man who had led them to this point.

"Benham?" Spencer asked, wanting to know if the senior case officer was okay.

Benham pulled his hand out of his jacket. It was covered in blood.

"Sanitäter!" Danny yelled, the German word for medic.

The BND medic rushed over to them as Spencer and Danny carefully helped the man to the ground.

"Looks like you found another device," Abbasi said, nodding toward the piece of wood and Semtex Spencer was still holding in his left hand. "Did you find the third?"

"There's another one down there?" Spencer asked, exhaustion evident in his voice.

"The guard we grabbed at the hotel confirmed there were three devices: one in the tunnel and two under the tracks," the injured spy confirmed.

"Don't worry, the Germans can finish looking for the third. Agent Hall had the BND turn on the signal jammers to ensure the devices couldn't go off. Saved all our asses with that decision," Danny said, looking at Spencer.

"The first device is in the tunnel, in a shopping bag on top of water pipes around the corner from the staircase that leads down to tunnel level," Spencer told them. "There is a canvas tool bag on the floor where I placed it."

"Not too bad for someone who didn't want anything to do with this case," Abbasi attempted to joke.
~~~

The German medic looked up from Abbasi’s wound and gave Spencer a quick nod to let him know he would be okay.

“Well, the guy was pretty committed to taking me out. He did blow up my hotel, after all. And you, being the consummate professional, had to go and take a bullet in the process. You realize you're CIA, not Secret Service, right?” Spencer joked with his friend.

Chapter 24

The team had finished its debriefing with the German Commander on the ground, and the BND field team had found the first device Spencer had disarmed, as well as the third one under the tracks.

A joint interrogation of the remaining terrorist they had captured at the hotel was being conducted by the Agency and the Germans to ensure they rounded up everyone involved in this network.

The CIA and the BND wanted to keep the truth about the Amir's identity from getting out to the public. It would not reflect well on the Americans to tell the world that the Amir had been dead for ten years, and it would not look good for the Germans for having allowed him into the country, plastic surgery or not.

However, the reality of an attempted terrorist attack by yet another radical Muslim group would cause additional uproar among German citizens. There would be more anti-Islamic protests in the days, weeks, and months ahead.

Abbasi had been taken to the TUM Klinikum Rechts der Isar hospital, just minutes away from the train station. It was considered the best hospital in Munich.

Spencer and Danny had arrived at the hospital shortly after their debrief with the Bundesnachrichtendienst.

Abbasi had one of the very few private rooms in the hospital, which were usually reserved for heads of state. There were two BND agents guarding the room to ensure Abbasi's safety.

Agent Hall was standing by Abbasi's bed, having a conversation with the injured man when Spencer and Danny walked in.

"I've put Charley in charge to finish the details of the case and report back to Langley."

"Congratulations, Kid. You've done a hell of a job."

"I had a good mentor," Hall responded.

"Yes, you did," both Danny and Spencer replied at the same time.

Agent Hall gave Abbasi a quick smile, one of reverence and appreciation, then turned to the other two men in the room, gave them a quick nod, and made his exit to get back to work.

"So, what now? You planning on retiring when you get out of here?" Spencer asked the man propped up in the hospital bed.

"I'd say it's about time. I've already contacted Langley and recommended Agent Hall to take the lead in the future. The kid proved himself and caught things I missed. I'd say he is ready."

"I'd second that motion," said Danny. "He has great instincts."

"What about you?" Abbasi asked, looking at Spencer. "You planning on heading back home?"

"My first plan is breakfast. I'm hungry enough to eat the ass end out of a dead rhino."

Spencer then looked at his friend, thinking back only a couple of days to their reunion at Danny's house and the guilt and shame he had felt. Both feelings had dissipated somewhat over the past couple of days.

A sense of peace was what Spencer felt now. He had regained the feeling he once had, thanks to his friends. A sense of belonging and now, a sense of gratitude.

"Then, I think I'll spend some time with family," he said, still looking at Danny.

"Sounds like a great plan to me," Danny responded. "Besides, I'll have hell to pay with Greta if you don't come back with me."

Epilogue

John Spencer awoke from a long, uninterrupted ten-hour night's sleep.

It was one of the most restful he had experienced in as long as he could remember.

The past several days had been very cathartic for him. First, the reunion with his friends, and then the conclusion of a decades-old mission, by killing the terrorist known as the Amir.

Spencer hadn't realized how void his life had been all these years. After he stopped feeling sorry for himself and laid off the booze, he got his head on straight and focused on the work.

He had accepted a job with the CIA and began his training. As a Case Officer, he had worked in the Asia Pacific area of operations and Europe.

After the Agency debacle in Tora Bora, and realizing that the higher-ups cared more about continuing the war than ending it, he left the agency behind. He was frustrated and tired.

Bedford Oil had given him the opportunity to take things easy. It was a lot of work, but mostly behind a desk. Compared to what he had done for the years before, it was a cakewalk.

Sure, he had had some casual relationships, usually with women wanting more than he was prepared to give. He had been burned once before, and that had been enough for him. John would not let someone else do that to him again. He had convinced himself he would be the consummate bachelor.

The discomfort he had felt for having walked away from his friends, Danny and Greta, had subsided to a degree. But he was sure he would never fully forgive himself for having done so, especially not for not being there to help when Greta was diagnosed with cancer.

She had always been like a mother to him, and he repaid it by walking away from the only genuine family he had ever known.

After coming back from Munich with Danny, the trio had spent a lot of time together, picking up where they had left off seventeen years earlier. The past week had done much to heal pieces of all three of them.

They talked in detail about their lives over the past decade and a half, reminisced about old times, joked about events they had all shared, and exchanged old war stories between Danny and Spencer.

A few nights earlier, Greta had asked John why he had never remarried. His response was immediate and rehearsed, something he had told himself for many years: never again.

"Aren't you lonely, John?" Greta had asked him sincerely.

He immediately wanted to tell her no. He was more than happy and brush off the idea of loneliness and family. Men like him didn't talk about such things and never admitted to it.

This time was different. Something inside him had changed over the past week.

"If I stop and think about it, yes. I am lonely. I've been guarded for so long, afraid of letting myself go through that again. I've just kept things casual and walked away when they went any further."

"Not all women are like her, John."

"I know," he said with a smile. "Look at you. You could never be like that." Then he stood up, gave her a kiss on the head, and left the room to find Danny in his workshop.

John had finished his shower and gotten dressed. He could smell the bacon coming from the kitchen. The past several days had given him a real sense of normalcy, what he imagined a normal family life was all about. And he liked it. He found himself thinking about it when going to sleep at night. Maybe, he thought. Maybe I'll give it another try if I meet the right person.

John made his way downstairs and into the kitchen.

"I could wake up every day for the rest of my life smelling you cook breakfast," he said, sitting at the table to pour a cup of coffee.

"I'll keep that in mind," came the reply as a hand set a plate down in front of him.

John was a bit shocked as he looked up at the beautiful dark-haired woman standing in front of him.

"I'm sorry. I thought you were Greta," John said.

"Don't be sorry. It's nice to have someone compliment the smell of my cooking. You may want to try it first, though," the woman replied with a jovial tone.

John sat there staring at the woman with a stupid grin on his face.

"Hi," the woman said, extending her arm to shake John's hand. "I'm Karen. Karen Moore. I take it they didn't tell you I would be here."

"Huh-uh," John replied, shaking his head and unable to take his eyes off the woman or the grin off his face. He was enamored.

"I'm a friend of Greta's and Danny's. I'm a doctor at the Landstuhl Regional Medical Center. I usually drive in once a month, spend the weekend, and help Greta around the house. Make sure her health is still good."

"Really?" John replied, still sitting there with a Cheshire cat grin on his face.

"Danny and Greta went to do their shopping in town. They should be back in a few hours. Now, eat your breakfast before it gets cold. If you're lucky, I might fix you lunch as well." She smiled and walked away to finish cleaning up the kitchen.

John grabbed a piece of bacon off his plate and took a bite, all the while watching the beauty who had just knocked him for a loop. Yes, John, I think it's time to try again, he said to himself with a quiet laugh. John Spencer sat at the kitchen table, eating his breakfast and drinking his coffee, and for the first time in his life, looked forward to what came next.

www.ingramcontent.com/pod-product-compliance
Lightning Source LLC
LaVergne TN
LVHW010702110826
845149LV00014B/3196

* 9 7 8 1 9 6 6 6 2 5 6 6 7 *